MW01135961

On a Wing and a Tear

Books for Young Readers by
CYNTHIA LEITICH SMITH

Blue Stars: Mission One: The Vice Principal Problem
(with Kekla Magoon)

Sisters of the Neversea

Ancestor Approved: Intertribal Stories for Kids
(contributing editor)

Indian Shoes

On a Wing and a Tear

CYNTHIA LEITICH SMITH

Heartdrum
An Imprint of HarperCollinsPublishers

Heartdrum is an imprint of HarperCollins Publishers.

On a Wing and a Tear
Copyright © 2024 by Cynthia Leitich Smith
Map art © 2024 by Natasha Donovan
All rights reserved. Printed in the United States of America.
No part of this book may be used or reproduced in any manner
whatsoever without written permission except in the case of
brief quotations embodied in critical articles and reviews. For
information address HarperCollins Children's Books, a division of
HarperCollins Publishers, 195 Broadway, New York, NY 10007.
www.harpercollinschildrens.com

Library of Congress Control Number: 2023948565
ISBN 978-0-06-287000-1

Typography by Andrea Vandergrift
24 25 26 27 28 LBC 5 4 3 2 1
First Edition

For Ellen Oh, with gratitude

CONTENTS

On a Wing and a Tear

1

ECHO OF THE PAST

Hesci, cousins! Looky there at that furry little guy, hugging himself in the hollow of an old oak tree. You hear his wet, steady snore?

That's Great-Grandfather Bat, *the* Bat, the one and only. The original, the bat who carries the mantle of winged-rodent sports history. Not Bat Leaf Nose or Bat Big Ears or even Bat Brown. Nope, we're talking about *Bat*, the famous ballplayer, sometimes called the Wings of Victory. The Animals herald him as a superstar, and the Birds do, too. Theirs is an age-old athletic rivalry—Team Animals versus Team Birds—stretching over eight hundred human generations. Maybe more! For all those years, Bat has been numero uno, the reigning MVP.

Not that the Birds are holding a grudge, mind you. After losing the Great Ball Game, the one talked about for generations, they were as gracious as they are graceful.

But my, oh, my, they've sure been longing for a rematch.

What's that, you say? Before your time? Huh. Maybe you're thinking there's not much more to Bat than his glory days—hanging upside down, making celebrity appearances, and surfing the breeze in the loving glow of Moon. But you'd best show some respect.

Bat is an Elder—as fast and strong as ever. Or at least he will be once that right wing heals up. What happened, you ask? Now, don't y'all fret. He has recovered, fine and dandy, from worse wing tears over the years and proudly shows off the scars to prove it.

This latest rip is teeny tiny—Bat caught his stretchy dark skin on the top of a chain-link fence. But we don't want it getting any worse now, do we? And he doesn't either. That's why Bat holed up all by his lonesome in the trunk of the nearest tree rather than risking the flight to snuggle with his kin in a crowded cave. He's cautious like that. It's one of the reasons he's lived so long. What's more, he was blessed by an act of neighborly generosity. From a nest in a walnut tree in the yard next door, Gray Squirrel had witnessed Bat's injury and his retreat into the oak. To help ensure his recovery, she'd scampered over a few times with gnawed-off scraps of a burlap shopping bag to line the hole in the trunk and keep him warm. Nope, she didn't have a clue that Bat was *the* Bat, but then again, it didn't matter. Gray Squirrel had been raised up right and understood the importance of looking after the community.

All of which is to say, so long as Bat stays put and doesn't aggravate the tear, our old friend is going to be just fine.

Fortunately for his recovery, the injury happened on a brief excursion toward the end of a mild winter, one of the warmest on record. This spring, when Bat crawls out of hibernation, he'll be rested, nearly healed, and almost ready for action. And that's saying something. Did you know that Bat can chow down twelve hundred bugs an hour and can travel faster than a hundred miles per hour? Fast enough to leave your uncle's rez truck in the dust.

Hey, have you ever gone walking in the woods? If so, you've probably heard the Birds and Animals sing songs of Bat—about how he's all heart, a multilingual eco-warrior, and a personal pal of Este Capko, who you might know as Bigfoot. Maybe you've heard Bigfoot sing songs about Bat, too.

Our friend Bat's got what you might call his Bat pride. Call his kin a "camp of bats," a "cloud of bats," or even a "cauldron of bats." But never, ever call them a "colony."

This is Bat's ancestral island, Bat's ancestral night skies. The bats made their home here long before y'all humans showed up. Yep, Bat is a wanderer, a wise and whimsical soul. He's also sure enough cozy, snoozing in that old oak tree in Chicago's Albany Park neighborhood.

Four weeks later, inside the red-brick bungalow on that same property, Ray Halfmoon was flipping pancakes for breakfast on the kitchen stove. It was less that he enjoyed cooking, and more that he enjoyed eating. You see, Ray was verging on a growth spurt and hungry much of the time. In the living room, Grampa Halfmoon relaxed in a worn recliner, catching up on Native Nations' and intertribal news on his phone as well as local news on the TV. Ray could hear the morning anchors talking about the rise and fall of lake levels, the risk of flooding.

Ray sent up a quick, quiet prayer of gratitude to the Creator for the glittery calm that morning in his own Albany Park neighborhood, partly bordered by the Chicago River and located to the northwest of the skyscrapers downtown. Outside, in front of his bungalow, street plows had pushed snow up two feet high, but that was business as usual for March in Chicago.

Once satisfied by his culinary efforts, Ray slid the final pancake onto the fourth plate, used fresh blueberries and strawberries to top it with a smiley face, and then grabbed an aluminum pot and wooden spoon. *Clang, clang, clang, clang!* "Come and get it!" Ray hollered—*clang, clang, clang, clang.* "Pancakes!"

"Stop that!" rang out houseguest Melanie "Mel" Roberts, covering her ears beneath a star quilt in the attic. *Clang, clang, clang, clang!* "It's Saturday, you monster!"

With a huff, Mel got up from the futon. *Clang, clang, clang, clang!* She'd been having that terrible dream again. The one where she was trying to bead, but she couldn't make out the colors, and all the beads were rolling away from her. *Clang, clang, clang, clang!*

Mel stuck her head into the stairwell. "That is so unnecessary!"

"But fun." Ray tossed the spoon into a spin and caught it one-handed. "Super fun." It's not like he'd always been a morning person either. In fact, Grampa's old nickname for Ray had been "Sleepybones." But to cut down on the before-school chaos of sharing the one bathroom, Ray had been getting up earlier to use it first.

Descending the attic stairs, Mel's mom grinned. "You'd think they'd always grown up together." She was a professor of education, someone who taught teachers how to teach, and she'd been grading college essays since dawn.

The Halfmoons were Cherokee and Seminole by heritage and citizens of the Cherokee Nation, which was located within the borders of Oklahoma. The Robertses were Muscogee, Odawa, and French-American by heritage and citizens of Muscogee Nation, likewise within Oklahoma. The families had hit it off last spring at the Dance for Mother Earth powwow in Ann Arbor, Michigan, when a filmmaker of the Tigua people of Ysleta del Sur Pueblo had interviewed both Grampa, who'd served in the army, and Mel's mom, who'd served in the coast guard, for a documentary film about Native military veterans.

Mel's mom rested a supportive hand on Grampa's shoulder. "You all right?"

Grampa lowered his recliner footrest, pushing up to stand, and Mel's tabby cat hopped onto his warm seat cushion. "It's this blasted, beautiful world we're livin' in. We're still fightin' to defend our land, and nobody else seems to know how to take care of it."

"Watch your screen time," she scolded gently. "There's a reason we limit the kids'." Both Mel and Ray had smartphones, but Mel's mom had used the settings to restrict their use of social media and other popular apps that she and Grampa had decided weren't healthy.

Last autumn, as the Robertses' lease was running out on their apartment in Kalamazoo, Michigan, Mel's mom received a last-minute offer to teach college in Chicago and, long story short, accepted Grampa's invitation for her and Mel to stay at his house. Mel had been grateful for a chance at a new beginning. She'd miss her auntie and little cousins in Kalamazoo, but ever since last winter, when Mel's best friend, Emma, moved to Lansing, Mel had felt like the odd one out at school. The fact that Emma's texts arrived less and less often over time hadn't helped any. The fact that her dad's texts and phone calls had gone from weekly to whenever was even worse.

By the time Ray began serving breakfast, Mel had joined them at the kitchen table and said the breakfast prayer: "Bless this mess. Amen."

"Amen," everybody said.

After slathering her pancake in maple syrup, Mel took a bite, savored the sticky sweetness, and told Ray, "You're forgiven for waking me up. This is epic! Stupendous! You're the best breakfast maker ever."

Ray laughed. "You're the best breakfast eater ever!"

Unfortunately, the grown-ups failed to fully appreciate

their joyful exchange. Despite the screen-time observation, both adults kept watching the TV news as they were eating. Finally, Grampa Halfmoon said, "This is a right-fine meal, Ray. Wado."

That afternoon, Grampa went grocery shopping with the Robertses, and now that Ray was in middle school, he was allowed to stay home alone with the pets for short periods of time.

On the family-room window bench, he made a video call to Aunt Wilhelmina in Cherokee Nation. Ray said, "Grampa says he likes to keep up with what's happening in the world, but a lot of the news is depressing. It wears on him."

Aunt Wilhelmina had her phone propped on the coffee table while she knitted a bright red-and-white scarf on the sofa. The flickering light from the stone fireplace played across her round, thoughtful face. Her fiftieth birthday was coming up and she was making scarves for the family and friends who'd be joining in the celebration. "Your grampa has a caring heart—you take after him that way. Give it time, Ray. He'll find something else to occupy his mind."

As Mel's tabby cat, Dragon, yawned on Ray's lap, Auntie added, "You do a good job of looking out for your Elders. But, hon, it's only natural that your grandfather gets upset about terrible things. It's when people *stop* caring that I worry." She tucked her knitting behind a throw pillow. "Art can be healing and offer hope. That's why I knit. That's why your uncle Leonard took up wood carving." A five-inch-tall figure of a wooden deer was displayed beside a handwoven basket on her coffee table. "Why don't you show me what you've drawn lately? Maybe one of your latest pictures could cheer up your grandfather."

Ray had given his grampa a lot of drawings and paintings over the years—the refrigerator was covered with them, and a few had been framed and hung in the hallway. But Ray knew better than to argue. So, he showed her his latest sketches of Dragon, of the soaring city skyline, and of Wrigley Field—where the Chicago Cubs played baseball.

A few blocks away at the grocery store, Mel pushed a shopping cart with a loose rear wheel through the produce aisle as her mother collected veggies—celery, carrots, and yellow onions—to make soup for dinner. What with the weather forecast, the place was hopping.

"Vitamin C!" Grampa Halfmoon exclaimed, plopping a bag of oranges in the wire basket. Technically, he was Ray's grandfather, not Mel's, but not to her Native way of thinking.

Satisfied by his gesture to nutrition, Grampa moseyed over to a pop-up tasting table. A middle-aged white woman wearing a dark-chocolate-syrup logo T-shirt and disposable clear plastic gloves greeted him with a smile, dipped a large strawberry in chocolate syrup, and offered it in a little white paper sample cup.

Grampa took a big bite, leaving only the little leaves at the top. "Delicious!"

"Fifteen percent off this week!" The table sales rep added, "We've got a backlog in the stockroom after Valentine's Day." She nodded toward Mel's mom, who was busy inspecting mushrooms. "Your wife might enjoy a sweet dessert. Or is that your daughter?"

Grampa shook his head. "More of a niece. I'm a widower. Lost my wife twenty-two years back. But I'm flattered you'd think of an old man like me as a dashin' romantic figure."

"Old man nothing." The lady tilted her head. "A lot of us appreciate a silver fox."

Mel gave her mom a knowing wink.

"Well, now." Grampa shuffled in his snow boots. "I . . . er, that is . . ." He was a striking figure with broad shoulders and long, graying dark hair in a braid. His warm, open demeanor attracted a fair share of admirers. But he tended to get flustered by romantic attention.

Recognizing the awkwardness, Mel steered the shopping cart close enough to the samples table so that she could add a bottle of the chocolate syrup. "This way, Fox. There's a snowstorm brewing, remember? We've got to grab our groceries and get home." As she led him away, Mel double-checked in a low voice, "You did want me to rescue you, right? You're not interested?"

"Right on," he said, thanking Mel as they moseyed to the bakery department, where her mom was picking out a loaf of sourdough bread. Grampa added, "Don't get me wrong. She was nice enough, but I've only been in love twice in my whole life, and I don't imagine that changin' anytime soon."

Twice? Mel thought. Still battling the loose wheel of the cart on the industrial beige tile, she couldn't stop herself from asking, "Your wife and . . . who?"

Grampa had a wistful look in his eye. "My high school sweetheart, a feisty girl named Georgia, from back home. She went off to college in Norman to become a teacher—an educator like your mama, only her specialty was science. About that same time, I went into the service, and over the years, we lost touch. She was a real firecracker, that one."

Mel blinked at the loaf of bread sailing into the basket to land on the oranges.

"Did you say *Georgia*?" As Mel's mom hurried over, she had her phone in her hand and her thumbs were flying on the tiny keyboard. "This is a long shot, but do you recognize this woman?" Mel's mom held up the screen to show a group photo taken at a roadside country restaurant.

Mel remembered that day from the previous summer. One of her mom's sorority sisters was getting married in Tulsa, and they had stopped in small-town Kansas to visit with cousins on the way to the wedding. Everyone called the woman "Aunt Georgia."

"Now, don't you get too excited." Grampa rolled his eyes. "There must be dozens of women her age named Georgia."

"Native women her age who are retired schoolteachers from Oklahoma?"

He glanced at the photo. "My Georgia wasn't a redhead."

"I doubt that's her natural hair color. Take a closer look. Was your Georgia from a Muscogee and Cherokee family?" Grampa's eyebrows went up, so Mel's mom used two fingers on the touch screen to enlarge the image and then handed her phone to him. "She and I hit it off over lunch, and a few months later, I ended up interviewing her for an article on tribal schools integrating Indigenous science into secondary classrooms."

He pursed his lips and adjusted his glasses. "Science, you say?"

Mel adored her mother, but sometimes she could be *quite* enthusiastic. Leaning in, Mel whispered, "Let's give him a little space."

Grampa trailed behind them—oblivious to the blueberry muffins, which were his favorites—as Mel and her mother rounded the corner to the meat counter. The Robertses took their time. While the butcher wrapped up flat-iron steaks for a young Black couple, Mel's mom picked up ground turkey and a whole bone-in chicken from the prepackaged display.

Like her mom, Mel had a low-key romantic streak, and

she brightened at the thought of a romance for Grampa. Swaying slightly to the watered-down pop music from the overhead speakers, Mel waved at a grinning, freckled toddler riding in a stroller pushed by his dad.

It wasn't until Grampa and the Robertses reached the eggs-and-dairy aisle that Grampa finally piped up in a warm voice. "I can hardly believe it, but I'd swear this *is* my Georgia!"

It was all Mel could do not to bounce up and down, clapping in the deli section.

"You don't say?" Mel's mom replied. "Well, as it happens, *your* Georgia is close with our cousins who live out west of Kansas City, near Haskell." She meant Haskell Indian Nations University in Lawrence, Kansas. "Georgia is retired now, but she runs a summer science-and-tech youth camp for Native teens in the area." With a chuckle, Mel's mom added, "She makes a memorable impression."

"I'm sure she does." Grampa quieted after that, and the trio hurried through the rest of their shopping, pausing to pick up thick egg noodles in the freezer section. He didn't say much as they waited in line with their fellow prestorm shoppers or as they checked out at the register or as they took small steps, walking like penguins, on the ice in the parking lot.

It wasn't until the groceries had been loaded in the hatchback and they'd all clicked their seat belts into place that Grampa finally said, "I can't tell from the picture if Georgia's wearing a wedding ring. I . . ." He rubbed his woolly beard. "I don't suppose you happen to recall?"

Wow, Mel thought. *He* is *interested.*

Her mom cranked the heater and turned on the wipers to clear the snow. "Widowed."

"That's a shame," Grampa replied in a weighty voice.

Shifting the hatchback into reverse, Mel's mom asked, "Is it?"

"Susan!" Grampa exclaimed, unzipping his jacket. "You're terrible!"

Mel muffled a burst of laughter with her mitten. Seated behind her mother, she watched his expression turn from vaguely scandalized to nostalgic in the front passenger seat. For a block or two, country oldies music from the radio filled the car, and then they started talking about spring break at the college where her mom worked and how it was scheduled later than the spring break at Mel's middle school.

The subject of Grampa's young love, Georgia, was dropped until the hatchback turned into the alley alongside the brick bungalow and he piped up, "Widowed how long?"

≈ 2 ≈

SPARK OF SPRING

Ray had his earbuds in, so he didn't hear everyone come home. It startled him when Mel threw open his bedroom door and exclaimed, "Guess what!" She didn't wait for an answer. "We're having chicken noodle soup for dinner—the kind with the thick, frozen egg noodles—and Grampa Halfmoon has a girlfriend."

Ray's ferret, Bandit, who'd been sleeping under a knitted blanket folded across the foot of the twin bed, yawned and roused himself to greet her. At the desk, Ray was putting the finishing touches on a drawing of Jack Frost skipping across clouds, surrounded by snow flurries. Ray made one more stroke of blue and set down his colored pencil and took out the buds, silencing the hip-hop music. "Did you remember cocoa?"

"Of course." Mel crouched to pet Bandit. "Did you not hear what I said?"

Leaning back in his desk chair, Ray replied, "Grampa

likes to watch the Cubs, go bowling with his army bud-
dies, take long walks along Lake Michigan, and attend
his Wednesday night Bible study group. He doesn't date,
and believe me, *plenty* of people at church have tried to
set him up. I've never heard him talk about any woman
romantic-like, except my grandmother. He does not have
a girlfriend."

"Ex-girlfriend," Mel clarified. That had sounded harsh
somehow. She tried again: "Former girlfriend." That was
better.

Ray wasn't impressed. "This former girlfriend must be
ancient history. Like Great Chicago Fire history, woolly
mammoth history, plesiosaur history—way, way back."

"Haven't you ever heard that history repeats itself?"
Mel asked, moving to sit on a braided rug. "Mom and I
know her. Her name is Georgia, she lives in Kansas, and
she's Grampa's high school sweetheart."

Kansas was a whole day's drive away, and when it came
to his grandfather, Ray had more pressing concerns than
decades-ago dating history. "I'm worried about him."

"Grampa Halfmoon?" Bandit climbed to her shoulder.
"Worried how?"

"He seems blah lately." Dragon slipped through the
doorway and circled Ray's ankles. "I mean, he's good
about taking his medicines and walking at the mall with
the Sneaker Seniors in the mornings. His bowling team
is on a winning streak. But Grampa pays a lot of attention to the news, and most of it is a bummer. I called my

aunt Wilhelmina today, and she says it's normal for people to be upset about bad stuff in the world. She says to give it time and he'll find something else to occupy his mind."

"Something like his long-lost young love?" Mel asked, waggling her eyebrows. She could be a lot sillier with family and closer friends than she was around other people.

"I salute your persistence." Ray showed her the artwork. "I drew that for him."

"Very cool!" she exclaimed. Across the bottom, he'd scrawled, *Get Lost, Jack Frost!* Clearly, someone had had enough of winter.

Of the two of them, Ray was the early riser with the can-do attitude. It could border on annoying, but Mel admired that about him. His optimism was contagious, and her spirit had felt lighter every day since moving in. "We should put more goodness into the world." A slow grin spread across her face. "Grampa's world. Even out the cosmic scales."

"Cosmic scales?" Ray put a rubber band around his colored pencils and set them next to his jar of loose change and folding money. "What do you have in mind?

As Bandit dived at Dragon, who dodged him and leaped onto Ray's bed, Mel said, "I've been thinking we could reconnect Grampa and Georgia. When her name came up today, he—"

"Hang on," Ray said, standing. Now Dragon was chasing Bandit, with pauses for play wrestling. "This Georgia person doesn't even live in Chicago. Besides, she's probably married."

"Nope, she—"

"What if she's dating someone?" Ray began pacing. "What if she's not interested in romance? Not everybody is, you know. What if she rejects him, and it breaks his heart?"

Mel understood that *Ray's* heart was in the right place. He and Grampa Halfmoon had been a team for a long time, and they were protective of each other. But suddenly all she could think about was her own parents' divorce, the fact that they didn't talk often, and that when they did, it was almost entirely about her. She didn't want to talk about heartbreak. She didn't even want to think about heartbreak. Ray read the flash of memory in her falling expression. He rushed to say, "Sorry. I didn't mean it like that. I should think before I open my—"

"It's okay." Mel's dad was busy with his new wife and her kids and a new manager job at his tribe's casino in northern Michigan. All of which was to say, Ray had a point. Grown-ups could be complicated.

"I know what you meant," Mel added, tossing a toy crinkle ball for Dragon and Bandit to chase across the hardwood floor. "You said yourself that Grampa could use some cheering up, and at the grocery store, there was a real spring in his step. But just in case, I'll check with my cousins first to make sure Georgia wants to hear from him."

* * *

17

As Mel and Dragon retreated to the attic, they could smell the chicken cooking in a big silver pot on the stove. Early on, Grampa Halfmoon had offered his own bedroom to the mother-daughter-cat trio, saying he'd be happy to bunk with Ray. But Mel's mom wouldn't hear of it, and the Robertses had divided the upstairs space with a makeshift half wall of wooden milk cartons that doubled as shelves. Those were mostly full of books—academic nonfiction for grown-ups and fantasy novels for young readers, plus a dozen or so realistic novels with Native heroes. The portion of the attic farthest from the stairwell was filled by their shared full-size futon, a hope chest, and a double dresser. Everything else was stored in Mel's auntie's basement back in Kalamazoo. All Mel had at her dad's place on the rez was an extra swimsuit, a beaded necklace, and a few changes of clothes.

"How's grading?" Mel asked as Dragon jumped up on the computer printer. "Will you be done in time for family movie night?" Given the incoming blizzard, the household planned to stay in and watch *Toy Story* movies, assuming the electricity didn't go out. Grampa had brought in extra wood for the fire and, as a backup plan, dug his Clue game out from the linen closet. They had gathered flashlights, candles, and extra blankets, too.

"Count on it," her mom said. "I'm stopping work at dinnertime, and if I'm not finished, I'll get up tomorrow morning before church."

"There's something else." Mel shifted her weight from one bare foot to another.

Her mom's fingers paused over the keyboard. "What's on your mind, Melanie?"

The answer came out in a rush. "Could you please give me Georgia's contact info so I can ask her about Grampa Halfmoon?"

"Hm." Raising an eyebrow, Mel's mom reached for the phone on her desk. "Officially, Elders are people, not projects. Unofficially, I'm texting Georgia directly."

Mel blinked. "Right now?" She hadn't expected things to move so fast. Mel drew closer to watch over her mother's shoulder.

"Right now. Hang on . . ." Mel's mom swiped away her texting app and clicked on photos. Another tap brought up a selfie Ray had taken of himself and Grampa riding the Ferris wheel at Navy Pier—with Lake Michigan rippling in the background. "What do you think?"

"I like it," Mel said. "They're laughing, happy. Out in the world. Grampa just went to the barbershop a few days before, so his eyebrows are behaving themselves."

Her mother added the photo to the text and read the draft aloud. "Hesci, Georgia. Melanie and I have become housemates with a widower named Charlie Halfmoon and his grandson in Chicago. Today we got to talking, and I believe you two may know each other from high school. Would you like to be put in touch with him?"

It never failed to fascinate Mel how long, complicated, and formal her mother's text messages were. Mel said, "Nice how you worked in that he's not married. Real smooth."

"Don't I know it." Her mother clicked send.

That blizzardy evening, after chicken noodle soup, followed by a rousing game of Clue—Ray won with "Dr. Orchid in the library with a candlestick"—Grampa Halfmoon was settled in his recliner, feet up, and using the TV remote to find *Toy Story 2* when his phone made a *ping* sound.

As he lifted it to check the message, Mel was carrying a bowl of warm, buttery popcorn into the living room, her mom was lounging on the sofa, and Ray was kneeling alongside the coffee table, putting the pieces of the board game back in their box. Dragon had curled up in front of the fire to warm her backside, and Bandit had retired for some personal time in his cage in Ray's bedroom. The latter was wholly optional, whether the rest of the household realized it or not. Like most ferrets, Bandit was a first-class escape artist and had become quietly adept at unfastening the latch. For a long time, he thought his name was *Ornery* because Grampa Halfmoon called him that so much.

Ping, Grampa's phone sounded again. "Excuse me." He lowered the footrest and stood up. "I'm going to my room."

Once he cleared out, Mel whispered, "Do you think that was Georgia?"

An uncertain look crossed her mother's face. "Do you think he's upset? Maybe I should've asked him first, before contacting her."

Mel set the popcorn on the coffee table. "On the way home from the grocery store, Grampa acted like he was really interested in her."

Ray was less sure. "He's never mentioned this Georgia person to me before."

It wasn't like Grampa Halfmoon to excuse himself in the middle of a family activity. Suddenly, they heard his voice, muffled by the closed door, from down the hall. Straining to listen, Mel picked up the TV remote from his recliner armrest, but she didn't press play. After all, it would be rude to start the movie without him. Ray reached for a handful of popcorn but reconsidered and withdrew. The lights flickered, and Mel's mom gently, quietly placed another log onto the fire. Rising flames crackled against the wood, and then they heard Grampa laugh—deep and wide and full of heart.

Mel's mom exhaled with relief, and Mel skipped across the living room to give Ray a high five. They laughed at themselves, at their playing matchmaker, and with delight that it seemed to be working.

What's that? You're worried about Great-Grandfather Bat?

Well, who could blame you? Cold can be fatal to bats.

That's why so many of them take refuge for the winter in caves and mines and garages. Nobody can blame y'all for fretting.

Take heart! The oak did its level best to shelter and protect. The burlap from Gray Squirrel added a layer of insulation, and Bat was no ordinary bat. He had a well-earned reputation for defying expectations. But what saved Great-Grandfather Bat that night was the burst of loving joy radiating from the Halfmoon bungalow.

It was so superb and summery that Great-Grandfather Bat felt it all the way through the red-brick walls and the white windy storm and the trunk of the tree in his cozy hidey-hole.

In that blessed moment, Bat became curious about the humans and their animal kin who lived in the nearby house. His well-honed instincts whispered that they were mighty fine folks.

☙ 3 ❧

BALL GAME

On a gray, cloudy morning a week and a half later, Ray and Mel bundled up and rode the yellow bus to Albany Park Mosaic Academy. Like their fellow three hundred or so students, they wore shirts in school colors—sky blue and lavender—with dark-colored pants. Skirts were an option, but neither Ray nor Mel much cared for them.

Their fellow students greeted them as they found their usual seats on the fourth-row bus bench, right side, with its view of the neighborhood business district, of the cracked sidewalks and local shops like Murphy Family Antiques and Chicago's Finest Deep-Dish Delights. Mel's stomach felt tight. "What if I freeze up? What if my slides look silly? What if Mrs. Flores gives me a bad grade?"

"Your report will be amazing," Ray replied, unzipping his puffy red vest. "Mrs. Flores will love it." As Mel opened her mouth to ask another what-if, he added, "You've got this. You did a great run-through last night in the living room. Stick to what you practiced; either look at your paper, the slides, or me, and you'll be fine."

"I'll be fine," Mel echoed. Even though she was still the new kid, Mel felt more confident at the academy than she ever had at her old school in Kalamazoo. Ray had been a big part of that. He wasn't popular in the way that Mel used to think of popularity, but everyone liked him. And ever since the first day, when Ray had introduced her around, all that goodwill had seemed to rub off on her. But fitting in had never come as easily to Mel.

An hour later, Mel stood at the front of Mrs. Flores's classroom, presenting her oral report for history class. Could anyone tell her knees were trembling? Could they see that her hands were shaking, too? Mel took a deep breath and slowly released it. "Today, I'm going to tell you about the Trail of Tears, the road to misery, and how my tribe rebuilt after that."

There! The opening had gone well. Last night's practice in the bathroom mirror had helped. Mel still felt vulnerable, exposed, with everyone watching, but there was no reason to panic. She checked the notes section of her presentation on the laptop screen to her right. She'd already listed everything she needed to say right there.

In the fourth row, Ray smiled and nodded once as if to say, *You've got this.*

Like she'd practiced, Mel took her time, gesturing on

occasion toward the slides shown on the screen behind her and then checking her notes again. She explained how, in the early-to-mid-1800s, President Andrew Jackson and the US Army had forcibly relocated her Muscogee ancestors and Ray's Cherokee and Seminole ancestors from their traditional lands in the southeast to Indian Territory, which was now the state of Oklahoma. She talked about the Muscogee Nation capital of Okmulgee and showed a slide of the tribe's district court in the Mound Building. She mentioned the Choctaw and Chickasaw, too.

"It's not the only example of something like that happening to Native peoples," she said. "Other tribal Nations, like the Ottawa Tribe of Oklahoma, were removed from their lands, too." Mel talked about the thousands of southeasterners—from Elders to babies in arms—who'd suffered and died along the way. As she spoke, Mel focused less on herself and on how she was coming across. What really mattered was speaking the truth so that the wrongs of the past could be addressed and because those long-ago Native people deserved their rightful place in history.

Mel made clear that the southeastern Natives had rebuilt their Nations and that they still remembered the tragedy today through paintings and stories and commemorative events like group walks and bike rides that retraced the journeys.

She kept to herself that while she'd been preparing her presentation, there had been moments when she'd felt her ancestors' presence—their support and encouragement, their strength and love.

Mel concluded, "Today, our Nations are surviving and often thriving. We're still here, and we always will be." At that, she exhaled and set the projector remote control on the roller stand. Her presentation was over. She'd done a terrific job! Her classmates burst into applause and hooted and hollered in appreciation, with Ray's voice being the loudest.

Spring break was right around the corner, and everyone was in high spirits.

Mel blushed at the attention. She was glad that Mrs. Flores trusted her students enough to let them pick their topics. Mel was less pleased about the upcoming question-and-answer portion of the assignment. If it weren't for that, her oral history report would be history itself.

Once the room quieted, Mrs. Flores stood from behind her desk. "Excellent job, Melanie! It's important for all of us to learn the history of Native peoples, which long precedes that of the United States. I also like how you used maps as visual aids. That was very effective."

"Native peoples *and Native Nations*," Mel said. Her hand flew to her mouth. Had she really dared to correct a grown-up? Her teacher? In front of the whole class?

"Native peoples *and Native Nations*," Mrs. Flores repeated, without missing a beat. "Yes, absolutely! An important point to remember. Thank you, Melanie."

As Ray gave Mel a thumbs-up, Mrs. Flores continued,

"Students, Melanie has educated us about landmark history *and* reminded us that this continent has always been populated with Native people and their tri—Nations. Does anyone have a question for her?"

A hand went up. Mrs. Flores called, "Jana?"

From the second row, Jana asked, "How are your old lands different from the new ones?"

Mel's brow pinched. "Well, the old lands are farther south . . . and east." Her presentation had already explained that—with visual aids. Mel tried to think of something less obvious to say and came up empty. "I don't know. I've never been to our Muscogee ancestral lands in the southeast. I didn't even grow up in Oklahoma, where the tribe is located now, though I've been to visit with my mom a lot."

Most Native people lived in cities, but sometimes she ached at the distance between her and her family, between her and her cultures. "I'm from Kalamazoo," she explained. "My dad's side of the family is Odawa, you know, from Michigan." There was more than one recognized Odawa tribe—her granddad was from Little Traverse Bay Bands and her grandma was from Little River Band, but right then, Mel decided not to get into all that. "So, I spend time with them on his rez, but not as much since my parents got divorced. Everything's different now. I mean, I still . . ." She was floundering. She hated floundering. "I, um—"

Mrs. Flores spoke up. "My family is Puerto Rican and

Polish, but I've never had a chance to visit Puerto Rico or Poland. Maybe someday." She scanned the room for another raised hand. "Does anyone else have a question?"

Ray had a couple of easy-to-answer questions ready, but Mel's nervous expression told him to hold his tongue.

"All right, then." Mrs. Flores gestured to Mel. "Let's hear it one more time for Melanie!"

Y'all, it was really something. On that very Thursday before spring break, Sun broke through the gray clouds to shine through Mrs. Flores's classroom windows. Mel had successfully shared her oral history report, and now she could relax and listen to everyone else's. The students cheered again. Mel returned to her desk seat, bumping her fist against Ray's, and thought about the ancestral homeland she'd never seen. *Maybe someday.*

After Jamal's report on President Barack Obama, Sharice's talk on the Great Chicago Fire, and Trinity's report on pilot Bessie Coleman, it was Ray's turn. His oral report was on the north Chicago baseball team. It was a well-timed choice. The season opener was a week away.

Ray bounced out of his seat. At the front of the classroom, he talked about the early names the club was known by, the legendary 1906 season, and how Wrigley Field was built in 1914. Ray mentioned the original scoreboard and how lights were installed in 1988. He highlighted famous players like Ernie Banks and passed on a few memories from his grandfather about watching Sammy Sosa. "Best of all, in 2016, the Cubbies finally won the World Series again! Like my grampa Halfmoon said, 'The icin' on the cake is that they clobbered a team with a disrespectful Indian mascot!'"

After Ray concluded his presentation, Mrs. Flores said, "Thank you! I'm a big Cubs fan, too. I'm so impressed that you interviewed your grandfather for the report. Way to go the extra mile! Class, always remember that your grandparents and the other senior citizens in your life were witnesses to history. They have fascinating stories to share. Any questions?"

Ray looked around the classroom. On the wall with the doorway, a bulletin board decorated with construction-paper tulips read, *How Does Kindness Grow?* Midway down the row of desks alongside it, Isaiah raised his hand. "Do you play baseball?"

"For sure! I'm on the same team as Dalton and Luis." Both boys brightened at the mention of their names. The first practice was next week, and Ray was looking forward to it.

In the middle of the front row, Ella raised her hand. "Does your grampa or anyone else in your family play baseball?"

Ray glowed with pride. "My dad played a couple of seasons for a minor league team in Oklahoma City. He was a third baseman."

Glancing at the wall clock, Mrs. Flores said, "We have time for one more before lunch."

Jack waved his hand from the far corner next to the

windows and the classroom library. "Does your dad still play?"

"My mom and dad died when I was a baby." Ray had said the words just like that so many times before that he automatically answered the typical next question. "They pulled over at a gas station off I-35 South, outside of Oklahoma City, and they got caught in a tornado. I'm the only one in the car who survived." Ray's best friends already knew that, though it wasn't something they talked about with him. They had been alerted by their grown-ups, who'd been told by Grampa.

Ray could feel the sympathy coming from his classmates, their horror at the thought of losing two parents at once, and their surprise that someone who'd once been called *a miracle baby* was a friend that they saw at school every day.

Mrs. Flores opened her mouth to comfort him, to take the pressure off him like she had with Mel. But Ray wasn't at a loss for what to say. "My grampa got me right away, and he has been there for me every day. He's told me so many stories about my parents that I feel like I know them. When we go to ball games together, it's like my dad is there with us."

"That's . . . that's lovely," Mrs. Flores said. "Thank you for sharing. Let's hear it for Ray, everybody!" As the applause grew louder, Ray added, "Let's hear it for the Cubs!"

* * *

That night, inspired by Ray's nonstop chatter about next week's ball game, Mel searched through her clothes in the attic. She found a Cubs baseball cap that belonged to her mom, but Mel's Cubs jersey felt too snug around the chest.

"You're growing up," her mom said, kneeling in front of their open antique trunk. T-shirts spilled out onto the hardwood floor. "There's still time. We can order you a new . . . no?"

Sitting on the futon, Mel was shaking her head. Ray's enthusiasm was infectious, and she wanted to go all out for the big day, but money was tight. Mel knew her dad sent a regular amount for child support, though he had a new family now, too. But her mom had remarked more than once on how much they were saving because Albany Park Mosaic Academy required school uniforms, so everyone wore matching pieces of clothing to school and—given that growing students changed sizes—the FFO (Families and Faculty Organization) coordinated twice-yearly resales. Mel said, "I'll go downstairs and ask to borrow a shirt."

"From Ray?" Her mother shut the lid. "Honey, I don't think his will fit—"

"From Grampa Halfmoon," Mel replied with a laugh. "I bet he has an extra Cubs jersey or T-shirt. It'll come down to my knees, but that's okay."

* * *

As Grampa Halfmoon had waved goodbye on his way to the bowling alley, he'd given Mel the green light to dig through his closet. She was doing just that when Ray strolled in. "Need help?"

Grampa had tightly rolled his casual shirts and stacked them in milk crates alongside his shoes and boots, neatly arranged on the top shelf of the closet. Mel was up on the kitchen step stool, stretching to reach. "Found one!" she exclaimed, tossing a shirt overhead for Ray to catch.

It was a white, striped replica jersey with the Cubs logo on the front and Banks 14 on the back in honor of the legendary Ernie Banks, Mr. Cub himself and one of the players Ray had mentioned in his history presentation. He said, "It'll be big on you."

"I can wear it with my red turtleneck and jeans," she replied, hopping to the hardwood floor as a hoarse, loud scream filled the night. *Kee-eeeee-arr! Kee-eeee-arr!*

"What was that?" Mel exclaimed.

"Outside!" Ray rushed to the window overlooking the backyard with Mel at his heels. He said, "It's a bird of prey—a falcon or a hawk."

They could make out a swooping, winged shadow, illuminated by the back porch light. "Hawk?" Mel whispered. "Falcon?" The raptor seemed to disappear, camouflaged by a cluster of barren brown branches. "Good thing Dragon is an inside cat."

Ray added, "Good thing Bandit is an inside ferret."

* * *

As you can imagine, Ray and Mel weren't the only ones startled by the full-throated cry of Red-Tailed Hawk. Inside the trunk of the old oak tree, Great-Grandfather Bat jolted awake.

Slithering snakes, ominous owls, and, yes, hungry hawks were among Bat's natural predators, but after taking a moment to compose himself, he refused to be afraid.

Bat had a long history of representing his kin at mixed-creature gatherings, including those between hunters and their natural prey, and Bat always fulfilled his duty with dignity. Besides, no self-respecting hawk would dare to harm an Elder of Bat's stature.

Still, Bat hadn't expected this disturbance to his rest and recovery. Imagine his surprise when he peeked out of the hole in the tree trunk and saw Cardinal instead. Red-Tailed Hawk was keeping a gracious distance farther up the oak, and Bat realized that Hawk must've been escorting the smaller red bird. Bat took it as a signal that they had arrived on official business.

"Great-Grandfather Bat," Cardinal sang. "I come bearing greetings and news from the Interspecies Athletic Community. May I please have a few moments of your time?"

Bat was no stranger to the IAC and appreciated his status as a Hall of Famer.

How many springs had come and gone since the Great Ball Game? Bat wondered. Was it already time to celebrate another anniversary? Careful to keep his injury hidden by the fold of his wing, Bat nudged aside the burlap fabric and, shivering, climbed halfway out of the hole in the trunk. "Welcome," he said. "I am Bat of Turtle Island. What can I do for you?"

Gray Squirrel had been scurrying down the length of a branch of the nearby walnut tree, within leaping distance of the chain-link fence connecting the two properties. She froze in place, tight against the limb, on heightened alert due to Hawk's nearby presence. You're right as rain that she shouldn't have moved at all, no matter how cautiously. But like most of her kin, Gray Squirrel was adventurous and a bit of a daredevil.

Cardinal said, "Great-Grandfather Bat, sir, I am pleased to inform you that a rematch game between the Birds and Animals has been scheduled for a week from today at the traditional playing field in the Southeast Lands before the Mighty Curved Shore."

"Rematch?" Bat echoed. "A week from today?" He felt a jolt of excitement and anticipation. As it so happened, Bat had grown weary of resting on his reputation. Sure, he enjoyed being a living legend, the surprise hero of the Great Ball Game. Who wouldn't? But it still chafed his backside whenever his buddy Robin teased that he'd caught the Birds off guard and that the win had been a fluke. A fluke! Can you imagine the gall of that bird?

Yes, indeed, Bat was raring for a rematch himself, if only to shut Robin's beak. But it wasn't as simple as that.

Normally, Bat could've made the long journey just fine, but his torn wing wasn't fully mended. On the upside, it would be healed in time for this upcoming game—*if* he kept resting it. Not that Bat was inclined to share his sticky situation with Cardinal. "Thank you kindly. I look forward to reuniting with my fellow Animals and y'all Birds, too."

Hugging the branch, Gray Squirrel could hardly believe her tiny ears. A rematch between the Animals and Birds? Talk about the thrill of a lifetime!

"May the best team win!" Cardinal said, taking flight with Red-Tailed Hawk.

"May the best team win," Bat muttered to himself, wondering how he was going to get most of the way across the continent. It was then that he noticed the glow from the back window of Grampa Halfmoon's bungalow and the two shadowy human pups peering out at the backyard.

❧ 4 ❧

WOUNDED WING

The next morning fell on the last day of school before spring break, which was also April Fools' Day. As usual, Mel's mom had already left home to ride the elevated train to her teaching job in the city, and Grampa had taken off for the indoor mall. As usual, Mel and Ray were bundled up and carrying their backpacks toward the bus stop in front of the Onsi house, just down the street. But what happened after that was anything but ordinary. "Hey, human pups!" called a squeaky voice in the distance. "Over here!"

"Did you hear that?" Mel asked, pausing on the cracked sidewalk.

The voice piped up again. "That's right, over here!"

"It doesn't sound human," Mel added.

Ray shifted the strap of his backpack. "It's coming from the side yard."

He was already jogging to investigate when Mel said,

"Wait! What if it's . . ." She hurried after him. "A bat. Is that a bat?"

It was. Great-Grandfather Bat was clinging to the outside of the chimney, past the fence gate and between the two windows on the side of the house. That's when Mel remembered what day it was. "Ray, it's a joke! An April Fools' joke." Mel was pleased that she'd figured it out so fast. "Grampa is trying to put one over on us."

Grampa Halfmoon was a kind soul, but many of us have a touch of trickster. Besides, a talking bat wasn't a mean-spirited trick. Odd, unexpected, but not mean.

Ray replied, "Grampa is on his way to walk at the mall with the Sneaker Seniors."

"Or that's what he wants us to think," Mel replied. Glancing down the street, she spotted their yellow school bus, turning the corner. "Ray, come on, we're going to be late!"

Of the two of them, Mel was the more academic one. It's not that Ray didn't enjoy school, but its appeal to him was mostly social. He was more interested in Indigenous cultural teachings, in his artwork, and in animals. Like ferrets and bats. He unlocked the fence gate, left it open behind him for Mel, and hurried to greet Bat. "Osiyo?"

Bat brightened. A youngster who knew the Cherokee word for *hello* had likely heard ball game stories before. "Osiyo! I am Bat of Turtle Island."

Ray's jaw dropped and his backpack slid off his shoulder, hitting the ground with a thud.

"Don't touch the bat," Mel said, hurrying to Ray's side. "It might bite you." She reached into her pocket for her phone. A few seconds later, she added, "The internet says if you find a bat in your home—"

"It's not in our home," Ray countered, still astonished. Mel continued scrolling. "Or if it's on the ground—"

"It's not on the ground," he pointed out. "And it *talks*."

They would sure enough miss the bus, Mel realized. But given that it was Grampa's fault, he could give them a ride to school when he got home from the mall—if he'd really left at all. Mel wouldn't put it past him to have doubled back to watch his shenanigans play out. But a couple of glances told her that Grampa wasn't peeking out the windows, and they hadn't been left open a crack to let in sound. Then there was the question of how the trick worked. Bat looked convincing. "It talks," she echoed. "Does it speak Mvskoke, too?"

"Hesci!" Bat shouted, and Mel took a giant step back. "Come now, pups!" Bat said. "We have a formidable journey ahead, and, due to an unfortunate injury, I require your assistance."

"You want us to help you?" Ray asked.

"You're hurt?" Mel's skepticism was dissipating. She had heard traditional stories about the Birds and Animals, even if none of them involved sixth graders in modern-day Chicago.

"I am in pressing need of traveling by one of your rolling or flying machines. If I'm to be fully recovered for the big ball game, I can't risk flying farther than very short distances."

Like all Birds and Animals, Bat had plenty of gripes with how most humans interacted with the natural world, but he had to admit they were an inventive bunch. They used tools even more than crows, sea otters, or dolphins, though at a far greater cost to the land, sky, and water.

Ray looked at Mel and gestured at Bat as if to ask, *How do you explain that?*

She couldn't. "Why is he calling us 'pups'? We're not dogs."

"I mean no disrespect," Bat insisted. "'Pups' is what we bats call our own young." Which, coming from Bat, made it a term of endearment.

Though most of the snow in the yard had melted, icy remnants of moisture on the grass seeped under the soles of Mel's black tennis shoes as she rocked slightly back and forth. She could hear the bus passing by, confirming that she and Ray had missed it. That said, neither one had any tests or assignments due that day. Enough grown-ups were taking their kids out of school early to travel over spring break that nothing major had been planned for any of their classes.

Bat was beginning to shiver. "Pups, you may accompany me to my roost in the oak tree or invite me into your brick one, but it is too cold to linger out here while you reconcile yourselves to the situation."

"Oh, I'm sorry!" Ray exclaimed, digging in his front

jeans pocket for his keys. If there's one thing that Grampa Halfmoon had made sure of, it was that his grandson had good manners. "Sure, come on into the house. I'm Ray and this is Mel . . . uh, also of Turtle Island. My people are from Cherokee Nation, and I have ancestors and family from Seminole Nation, too."

When Mel hesitated to chime in, Ray added, "Mel's people are from Muscogee Nation in Oklahoma, but her dad's side of the family is Odawa."

"Yep, we're talking to a bat." Mel threw up her hands. "I swear, at this point, we might as well be Indigenous animations."

Ray retrieved his backpack, turned to the side, and tapped a hand on the puffy red vest covering his own shoulder. "Here! You can hitch a ride with me. Bandit— he's a ferret—does it all the time."

"Wado! Mvto!" Bat said. "You are exceptional!" Not wanting the more reticent Mel to feel bad, he added, "So are you, pup!"

As Bat glided to Ray's shoulder, Mel exclaimed, "You are not supposed to touch a bat!"

"I'm not supposed to touch a human either," Bat replied matter-of-factly.

Inside the bungalow, Dragon's eyes dilated at the sight of Bat. She arched her back, hissed, and retreated backward at a sharp angle before skulking up the attic stairs.

"Dragon!" Mel scolded. "How rude!"

"There are a few shoeboxes in the basement," Ray said to Mel. "Could you go down and grab one?" As she left, Ray made his way to the kitchen. "Would you like something to drink?"

"Water, please," Bat said, delighted but not surprised by the hospitality. Bat had always considered himself an excellent judge of character.

Ray used the internet browser on his phone to learn that bat rescuers used something he had in supply—clean paintbrushes—to offer water to bats. But given Dragon's outsize reaction, Ray was reluctant to introduce Bat to Bandit. "Why don't you hang out over there?" Ray moved to the fireplace mantel in the adjacent living room. "I'll be right back."

That sounded dandy to Bat. He'd already taken a liking to the pups. Bat crawled from the shoulder of Ray's puffy red vest to his new resting place and surveyed his surroundings. The inside of the pups' roost was longer than it was wide, but Bat had noticed that from the outside. It was filled with soft landing places, nooks, and crannies. Plenty of places for a bat to hide. He'd heard of his kin taking refuge in human dwellings, which usually turned out to be a bad idea.

Humans could be more territorial than wolves.

When it came to canines, Bat was mighty impressed with the fluffy Pomeranian on the block who'd weaponized his upturned brown eyes to fully control humans. Bat's intentions with the residents of the Halfmoon bungalow were nowhere near so lofty. He didn't want to roost with them permanently. All Bat needed was a ride . . . and, more pressingly, due to the presence of a cat in the house, to find higher ground. Cats might not be able to fly, but they had impressive vertical leaping skills. The green curtains to either side of the front window looked promising.

A moment later, Grampa Halfmoon, who'd forgotten his wallet, moseyed through the front door in his mall-walking sneakers. Mel emerged from the basement with a shoebox, and Ray appeared from the hallway with a new paintbrush.

"Hey, kids! What're y'all doing here?" Grampa asked. "Your spring break doesn't start until next week. Shouldn't you two be off to school right about now?"

"It's a long story," Mel said.

Ray put in, "On our way to the bus stop, a bat called out to us from the side of the house. He said he needed our help. But he was cold, so we came inside to talk about it."

"Or not that long of a story," Mel amended.

Moving toward the fireplace mantel, Ray called, "Where did the bat go?"

"What do you mean?" Mel asked. "You're the one who was carrying it on your shoulder."

"A bat, you say?" Grampa Halfmoon walked in, scanning the room. Ray's and Mel's backpacks had been left on the floor of the entry. Dragon hadn't greeted Grampa at the door, but otherwise, everything seemed normal. "You brought it into the house? Is it injured?"

"How did you know?" Bat exclaimed from atop the green curtains. He bobbed his furry head up and down, studying the familiar-looking Elder. "Charlie Halfmoon, is that you?"

"Bat!" Grampa exclaimed, slipping off his gold cap and denim jacket. "Old friend, it's been years! My goodness! You're lookin' handsome as ever. What brings you to Chicago?"

"Who'd have imaged I'd run into you here?" Bat said.

"Well, it is my house," Grampa replied, and they both laughed.

How bizarre, Mel and Ray thought at the same time.

Bat explained, "I was on a northern tour, visiting the local bat communities, when my wing got caught on a chain-link fence. I've been roosting in an oak out back for over a full moon cycle." Bat laughed again. "Talk about a coincidence!"

"I don't believe in coincidences," Grampa Halfmoon replied, lighting the gas fireplace. "This here is part of the Creator's plan. What can we do for you?"

"It's a big ask," Bat replied, fluttering to the armrest of Grampa's recliner. "I'm supposed to be more than halfway across Turtle Island in less than a week."

"Less than a week?" Grampa Halfmoon rubbed his beard. "And that sounds like quite the distance." He squared his broad shoulders. "Don't you worry none. I don't think the TSA would take kindly to me sneaking a bat onto an airplane, but after all the good you've done for me, I promise we'll figure out how to get you where you need to go."

Ray and Mel broke into wide grins. Mel took off her jacket and made herself comfortable on the couch while Ray filled a paintbrush with water for their visitor and put on a pan of milk to make cocoa for the rest of them. Mel still wasn't entirely sure what to think, but she had all the faith in the world in Grampa.

Bat wasn't much of a day dweller. After sipping some water, he showed Mel and the Halfmoons his injury and relayed what Cardinal had said about the rematch between the Birds and Animals on the traditional playing field in the Southeast Lands before the Mighty Curved Shore.

"Wait a minute!" Mel said, setting her steaming mug of cocoa on the coffee table. "You're *that* Bat? The one who won the Great Ball Game?" She had heard the traditional story from a beloved great auntie, the one about how the other Animals had said Bat was too small to affect the outcome, but Bat had won the game by flying high and using his teeth to catch the ball.

"Is there a dispute y'all are hopin' to settle?" Grampa asked. "The Birds and the Animals, I mean?" He was lining the shoebox that Mel had brought upstairs with a rectangle of thin plastic cut from a trash bag, which he attached at the corners, and, on top of that, he placed a couple of folded paper napkins for cushioning, and a clean cotton tea towel embroidered by Aunt Wilhelmina. After all, Bat was an honored guest and deserved the very best.

"It's more of a good-natured rivalry," Bat explained from the rim of a decorative bowl of pine cones near Mel's mug. Bat gulped a final chunk of Dragon's meaty canned food from a saucer, keeping a wary eye out for the cat herself.

"Birds versus Animals," Ray said, confused. "Aren't birds a type of animal?"

"With feathers, not fur!" Bat exclaimed as though that explained everything.

Ray restrained himself from asking about Bat's thoughts on fish, reptiles, and amphibians. He might not agree with everything his Elders said, but he knew better than to press them with questions without good reason.

Mel slid off the couch to sit closer to Bat. It was rude to stare, but she couldn't help herself. "How is it that you can talk to people?"

Both Bat and Grampa Halfmoon chuckled. Grampa placed the box on the table for easy entry. "How do you think we humans learned about Bat and the ball game in the first place?"

Bat added, "Most animals can talk to each other, and a few of us can talk to humans." He yawned. "Raccoon brags that all his kin speak Anishinaabemowin."

From the attic, Dragon slinked down to the third stair from the top to study Bat's every move. As fate had it,

Dragon had been separated from her mama before she could learn all the ways of the Animals. She was able to understand that Bat was communicating with her humans in their language but could only decipher a few words. Bandit could've helped translate, but he was still in his cage in Ray's bedroom. So, her main takeaway was that a flying rodent in her house was eating what smelled like her breakfast.

Having left Bat snoozing in the shoebox on his night-stand, Grampa Halfmoon drove Mel and Ray to school. Grampa said, "I suppose we could overnight mail Bat to the Gulf Coast. I'm acquainted with a fine Poarch Creek fellow in Alabama who'd probably be able to take him the rest of the way to the traditional playing field. But packages get lost every day. I'm not comfortable taking that kind of risk with Bat."

"The Gulf Coast is huge," Mel pointed out from the back seat. *Huge* was an understatement! Consider Florida to the east, Texas to the west—Louisiana, Mississippi, and Alabama in between. However, considering Bat's mention of the Southeast Lands before the Mighty Curved Shore, it seemed safe enough to rule out Texas and, to the south of that, Mexico. "Grampa, do you know exactly where this traditional playing field is located?"

"Nope." Grampa Halfmoon checked the mileage on his truck, wondering if he could get it into the shop that afternoon for a tune-up. "Our good friend Bat will have to point the way."

"Road trip?" Ray plugged locations into the map app on his phone. "If we're thinking Mississippi, we could make the round trip in about twenty-four hours. If it's Louisiana—"

Grampa Halfmoon slowed at the four-way stop next to Chicago's Finest Deep-Dish Delights. "Hold your horses! A body's got to sleep, and it's not smart to push too hard with highway driving. I figure three or four days down, three or four days back, depending on the weather." He patted the steering wheel. "Assuming this old truck is feeling cooperative."

Ray felt a flash of panic. "The Cubs season opener—"

"Is Thursday," Grampa said. "I know, Ray. I know. I'm sorry I'll have to miss out on our tradition this year by not going with you to the game. Pains my heart, too, but Bat came to us in need, and we can't let him down."

"What about Ray and me?" Mel asked. Next week was spring break, after all.

Grampa felt torn. He needed to help his good friend Bat—no question about it—but he hated the thought of disappointing Ray. "Your mom will be downtown teaching," he said to Mel. "Maybe you two kids could spend a few days with the Wangs or the Wilsons."

Do y'all remember Ray's friends from Mrs. Flores's class? Dalton Wang and Luis Wilson? Grampa Halfmoon was talking about their families. Normally, Ray would've been glad to spend a week with either one. But this wasn't a normal situation. "Going to the Cubs season opener is *our* tradition," Ray said, cringing at the whine in his voice. Whining never got him anywhere with his grandfather. It wasn't that Ray couldn't be flexible. He'd been happy about the prospect of Mel joining them for the baseball game. Dalton and Luis had tagged along before, too. But *Grampa* had to be there. Didn't he?

5

ROAD TO GEORGIA

Ray and Mel had library period at the end of that school day. Students were welcome to study at the table of their choice, use the computers, or browse the shelves. Mel said, "I'm not sure it's okay for Bat to eat Dragon's food."

"He seems to like it," Ray replied. The internet had said that meaty cat food was fine for rescued bats, but Mel was the bookish type.

"We like chocolate-caramel popcorn," she replied. "But it's not good for us. And Bat needs all the nutrients he can get to heal up in time to play the big game." Lingering a moment at the new books display, she snatched up the latest in her favorite fantasy series. "If we can show that we're responsible enough, maybe Grampa Halfmoon will take us on the trip."

"You want to leave town with Grampa? And miss the season opener?" Was she trying to bail on him, too?

Mel knew that Cubs tickets were pricey—as in

save-up-all-year pricey. But plenty of folks would be happy to go in her place. Besides, she'd always had a soft spot for Elders and animals, and the journey would involve spending quality time with both. "If Grampa Halfmoon and my mom say I can. Ray . . ." Mel understood that his love of baseball went deep—it was tied to his relationship to the dad he'd never known. "I want you to come, too."

"Me? What about—"

"There will be other spring practices with Dalton and Luis, other Cubs games, even other season openers. Besides, the rematch between the Birds and Animals is a ball game, too, and not just any ball game. It's epic! This trip is a once-in-a-lifetime opportunity!"

Ray weighed Mel's words. Much as he loved the Cubbies, she'd made some good points. He thought it through. If they were road-tripping southeast, Ray could expect to stay with Aunt Wilhelmina and Uncle Leonard in Cherokee Nation. Growing up, Ray's dad had spent most summers with them and his cousins, fishing at the nearby lake. If there was one place besides Wrigley Field that Ray felt especially close to his father, it was back home in Cherokee Nation. Plus, if that's where Grampa Halfmoon was, then it was where Ray wanted to be, too. Suddenly, he was struck with the conviction that his dad would've wanted him to go. He briefly let himself mourn the planned day at the ballpark and then let that go. The emptiness left behind quickly filled with anticipation as

Ray turned his attention to his new goal. "How do we make our case?"

Elated by his change of heart, Mel skipped across the globe-design rug to the nonfiction display labeled *Our Animal Relatives*. She said, "Bat originally called out to us for help from the side yard. It was *you and me* that he was waiting for on the chimney brick when we were on our way to the bus stop this morning. Bat didn't know then that his old pal Charlie was the man living in the house. He chose us. He must've thought we were capable." Scanning the forward-facing books, she picked up *The Handy Pocket Guide to Bats*. "If we show we're taking that seriously and we've done our homework, our grown-ups might be more willing to say yes."

Ray took the bat guidebook from her and began leafing through it. "Uh, Mel?" he began, his voice rising in alarm. "We better text Grampa Halfmoon. It says here that house cats are known to hunt and kill bats!"

Her eyes widened. "Dragon!"

At the Halfmoon bungalow, Grampa had left his phone on the kitchen counter and ducked into his bedroom to check on Bat. He was surprised to find Gray Squirrel on the opposite windowsill, barking through the antique glass.

"There you are, Charlie!" Great-Grandfather Bat said. Until today, he hadn't realized how lonely he'd been, holed up in the trunk of the oak tree. All this socializing—Cardinal, the human pups, his friend Charlie, and now Gray Squirrel—it lifted Bat's spirits considerably. "Could you please open the window? Our neighbor here would like to have a word with me."

"I'd say so!" Grampa Halfmoon exclaimed. This was usually the most peaceful and quiet room in the house. It was sparsely furnished, except for the bookcase overflowing with nonfiction books about military history, Native history, and Native military history. The only standout decor was a framed vintage poster for a Chicago ballet company.

After Grampa opened the window, Gray Squirrel chirped, slipped inside, and placed a pecan in his palm as a show of gratitude.

"Welcome, little one," Grampa Halfmoon said to the squirrel. "I'll leave y'all to your business. I'm goin' to shut this for now, so we're not heatin' up the whole outside. Just let me know when you'd like to leave." As he departed, Grampa left the bedroom door open behind him, so he'd hear the animals call out when his assistance was needed.

Grampa Halfmoon's hospitality didn't surprise Gray Squirrel. Grampa regularly refilled outdoor feeders for squirrels and birds and even a special red one for the hummingbirds every spring once the weather warmed up. His gardens beckoned bees and butterflies, and his patio featured an elevated concrete drink-and-splash station. Y'all may have heard it called a fountain.

Still, Gray Squirrel marveled at the summery tempera-ture inside the boxy human nest. Gray Squirrel was young and starstruck but also brimming with questions. Her ear-liest memories of Mama Squirrel were intertwined with the story of Bat's moment of victory.

"Great-Grandfather Bat," Gray Squirrel began. "Please forgive this interruption into your slumber. Thank you for speaking with me. I—I . . . I may have overheard . . ." Gray Squirrel paused, composed herself, and fluffed her tail to its full glory. *Overheard* may have been an under-statement, but she didn't want to open the conversation by admitting to eavesdropping. "Um, I overheard Cardi-nal informing you of a rematch game between the Birds and Animals. I have come to wish you luck."

Bat was charmed. "Thank you, Gray Squirrel. I'll do my humble best."

As Gray Squirrel beamed at him, Bat thought it over. Should he continue trying to hide his wing tear? For countless generations, squirrels had valiantly accepted the responsibility of sharing important communications among the Animals. Should he ask Gray Squirrel to reach out to the Nuts News Network and announce the game, mentioning his injury? Might that make the Birds over-confident of their chances of victory? Or might his Animal teammates despair at their prospects? He decided to keep it all to himself for the time being. You never knew how a story might shift once you set it loose in the world. In any case, Bat's wing was nearly fully mended. He prayed it would be at 100 percent by game day.

After getting to know Gray Squirrel better, Bat began retelling the story that had made him famous. "Ours is an age-old sports rivalry—Team Animals versus Team Birds—stretching back millions of squirrel generations. . . ."

Gray Squirrel hung on every word. Imagine hearing the age-old tale from its hero!

Down the hall, Bandit yawned in his cage, having been awakened by the creaky hallway floorboard beneath Grampa Halfmoon's departing footsteps. He didn't think much of that. Bandit had sensitive ears, and the humans tended to disturb his afternoon naps. But Dragon did catch Bandit's eye as she slinked—not sauntered, per usual—past Ray's bedroom doorway.

In contrast, the same mysterious guest who'd created such a fuss that morning was having a boisterous conversation down the hall with . . . what was a squirrel doing inside Bandit's territory? What did Dragon think she was going to do about it?

At times, Bandit had longed for the company of fellow ferrets and sometimes dreamed of hunting rats, rabbits, or squirrels, but his indoor den was luxurious, and his young human companion was diligent about ensuring he never went hungry.

Bandit considered himself a debonair ferret of leisure. Still, this was getting ridiculous. These animals—plural—had invaded his territory. It was one thing when Dragon had moved in and claimed the attic, which was mostly outside Bandit's area of interest, and the feline made a fun playmate. Besides, the cat came with her own human caretakers. Bandit's household had remained in balance, and it was a more entertaining place to be. This latest development, on the other hand, tempted chaos. Or, at the very least, merited investigation. Resolved, the ferret rose from his bedding and jostled the latch of his cage loose. He hurried out of Ray's room and down the hall, past the bathroom.

As the tabby's nose and whiskers peeked out from beneath the quilt covering Grampa Halfmoon's bed, Gray Squirrel barked, "Cat! Cat! Cat! Cat!"

Bat soared to the top of the tall dresser. Dragon leaped at Gray Squirrel, who darted past her and ricocheted off the headboard. Dragon's claws scrambled to no avail on the windowsill, and, losing her balance, she twisted, midair, to land on a braided rug. Meanwhile, Bandit scaled the far nightstand, continuing to the top of the lamp, and cried, "Enough mayhem! What are you"—he addressed Gray Squirrel on Grampa Halfmoon's pillow—"and you"—he addressed Bat, who had inadvertently revealed his torn wing—"doing in my territory?"

Dragon crouched on the rug, tail swishing. She had a

companionable relationship with Bandit, a fellow predator and a proud member of the weasel family. Her goodwill did not extend to bats or to squirrels. It was, after all, her sworn duty to dispose of nuisance rodents. But she was willing to listen to her friend. Suddenly, the young humans burst into the room, closely followed by their Elder. In a blink, a small blur of gray vanished behind the curtains. That infernal squirrel!

"Dragon!" The girl rushed around Grampa's bed to unceremoniously scoop up the cat.

"Bat! Are you hurt?" Grampa Halfmoon called, scanning the room. "Or hurt worse?"

"I am safe, old friend," Bat assured him, having hopped up from the dresser to hang upside down from the curtain rod. "A riotous scuffle, but fortunately, no one was harmed."

Ray reached for Bandit. "Looks like we got here just in time!" he said, which struck the ferret as deeply presumptuous, as he'd already had the crisis well in paw.

It was decided that Dragon would be "more comfortable" sequestered in the bathroom until Bat was safely on his way. However, Bat spoke up on Bandit's behalf, and so the ferret maintained his roaming privileges. Bandit pretended that, like Dragon, he was ignorant of the human language. He considered it his personal business.

That settled, while Bat and Gray Squirrel resumed their conversation in Grampa's bedroom, the humans reconvened at the kitchen table, where stories were shared and decisions were made. Mel pulled out a chair for the Elder to sit. "Would you like a mug of cocoa?"

Grampa Halfmoon raised an eyebrow. "You tryin' to butter me up, little girl?"

"She wants us to come with you to take Bat to the rematch ball game," Ray put in.

"Ray!" Mel exclaimed, hands on her hips. "That, that is not even a question." She slid into her usual seat at the table and leaned into her manners. "Grampa Halfmoon, may Ray and I accompany you and Bat to the traditional playing field?"

Grampa was pleased but not too surprised by the question. He patted her hand. "I'd be honored by the company, so long as your mama says it's okay." Turning to Ray, Grampa added, "You'd be willing to miss your baseball practice?" At the firm answering nod, he added, "And the Cubs' season opener?"

"Yes." Ray exhaled. "I've thought about all that." He nodded at Mel. "We talked about it. The trip would mean a visit to Uncle Leonard and Aunt Wilhelmina's, right?"

"Of course," Grampa Halfmoon said. "Her birthday's coming up, you know. Even if we miss the exact date, we could all celebrate it together in person."

That joyful thought was a bow on Ray's decision. "I'm in."

"This shows a real maturity. You're livin' your values." Grampa Halfmoon leaned back in his chair. "I'm proud of you. Both of you."

* * *

When Mel's mom arrived home with a take-out deep-dish pizza to celebrate the beginning of spring break, she took Bat's request for aid to heart. There was only one sticking point. Sprinkling red pepper flakes on her slice of pepperoni pizza, she said, "Thing is, Charlie, humans aren't supposed to touch bats. They can carry rabies. Kids, did you touch Bat?"

Mel and Ray shook their heads. "Bat hasn't tried to touch our skin," Ray said. "He came into the house on the shoulder of my winter vest, and we can carry him in the shoebox."

Grampa Halfmoon gestured at *The Handy Pocket Guide to Bats*. "I figure he's an exception to a lot of what you'd find in that book. Susan, there's no need to fret."

Under the table, the balls of Mel's feet were bouncing on the tile. In her most serious, grown-up voice, she said, "Mom, we'll never ever touch a bat unless it's a famous sports star and only with its consent. We promise."

Her mom responded with equal seriousness. "No one would ever guess you're a professor's child. All right. Mel, I hereby officially green-light your road trip. I'll need to run it by your father, but I seriously doubt he'll object."

Her dad had made a point of meeting the Halfmoons before the big move to Chicago, but he almost always went along with her mother on parenting decisions. Mel hoped it was a sign of his trust and agreeable nature, but sometimes her texts to him went unanswered, and she wondered how much he cared.

"We can give our Cubs tickets to my friends Dalton and Luis," Ray began, wiping stringy cheese from his chin. "Do you still want to go?"

"I'll have plenty of grading to do here," Mel's mom replied. "But if they end up with an extra ticket, maybe I'll take a break that day." She got up to refill the pitcher with ice and tea that had been steeping on the stove. "Charlie, are you sure the truck can make it that far? Would you rather take my hatchback? Or maybe you could get bus tickets and rent a car once you—"

"Great-Grandfather Bat generally doesn't travel by highways, let alone bus routes," Grampa Halfmoon said, tearing off two fresh paper towels to use as napkins and then ripping each in half to share. "With Bat acting as our navigator, we'll need to be as flexible as possible. It'll be confounding enough for him, traveling so close to the ground."

In Grampa Halfmoon's bedroom, Bat found himself in a trickier situation than he'd been in before the cat had so rudely interrupted. Now, Gray Squirrel knew about the wing injury Bat had been so careful to hide. Truth was, it wasn't just the danger of rumors or fallout of his celebrity image or any restrictions that might be imposed by the Interspecies Athletic Community. Like most living creatures, Bat had always been careful not to project weakness. In a world of predators and prey, that kind of vulnerability could spell doom.

He chose to remain where he was, upside down, wings tucked in, hanging from the curtain rod. After such a close call with Dragon, he might well stay up there all night.

"Great-Grandfather Bat," Gray Squirrel began, illuminated by the stained-glass shade of a standing lamp, "I'm so, so sorry that I put your safety at risk. I fear my presence may have attracted that vile cat. I've seen her, scowling out from this human nest, and she is even more despicable than I imagined." As you might well imagine, especially among younger animals, certain misconceptions and, yes, even stereotypes persisted, and given their opposing goals—house cats to hunt and squirrels to survive—occasionally, there were hard feelings.

Upon reflection, Bat conceded to himself that perhaps a rematch between the Birds and Animals was a good idea. Between habitat loss, climate change, and disease, tensions over hunting were steadily escalating. It wasn't only in this human roost that nature was out of balance. The rematch would be a healthy, cathartic distraction. Aquatic animals, who engaged in conflict-resolution traditions of their own, tended to minimize the stakes of the land sports as "bragging rights," even if they did send members of the otter, turtle, or crocodilian families to bear witness and report back. However, ball games had a long history of heading off serious confrontations while building friendships and understanding. Many of Bat's fellow ballplayers were less circumspect—Turkey and Wolverine, for example. Bat imagined that news of such a headline sporting event was already spreading in all four directions.

"Young one," Great-Grandfather Bat replied. "That wasn't the first house cat I've faced, and if the Creator is willing, it won't be the last." For the record, Bat had also experienced a few near misses involving owls, hawks, coyotes, and one precocious, bad-tempered grackle. "No apologies are necessary."

"Thank you," Gray Squirrel said. "And please forgive me, but I couldn't help noticing the tear in your wing." Out of respect, Gray Squirrel didn't press beyond that. Her ears flickered, though, ready for his answer.

"And I couldn't help noticing how observant you are," Bat replied. "Your warning about the cat may have saved my life, and I must say I'm impressed by your manners. Tell me, Gray Squirrel, what do you think about coming along with us to the big game?"

Gray Squirrel's tail flicked with joy. A historic journey, with a famous athlete on the mend as each sunset brought him closer to defending his proud sports legacy? "Yes!" she exclaimed, zipping in circles on top of the bed. "Yes, yes, yippee!"

Bat had taken a liking to Gray Squirrel, but she could be exhausting. Especially, he realized, on a multiday road trip, but he felt honored by her friendship and valued her kind and loyal heart.

Before bedtime, Mel's mom brought her laptop down to the TV in the living room. Again, Bat had seen his share of human tools and, for that matter, the toll they took on the natural world. As he'd learned from zoo visits, orangutans made whistles out of leaves and elephants modified branches into fly swatters. From word of mouth on jaunts to the oceans, he'd found out that some octopuses used discarded coconut shells to make armor and shelters. Yet none of them spewed poison into the water or skies. None of them destroyed or hoarded land, sky, or water that since the beginning of everything had been respectfully shared. Well, mostly shared. Tempers could run high during breeding season and in the face of threats to territory or one's young.

That said, having been relocated to the decorative bowl of pine cones on the Halfmoons' coffee table, Bat purred thoughtfully at the satellite aerial imagery that filled the screen. "This is Chicagoland," Mel said, pointing. "The whole metro area."

Bat nodded, intrigued but mystified. "Chicagoland?"

"This huge human settlement," Grampa Halfmoon clarified. "Where we are now. The picture on that screen is from outer space. Way up above the clouds, in the stars."

"In the stars!" Bat exclaimed. On countless occasions, he'd observed human flying machines in the sky. Noisy nuisances. Who would've imagined they could travel so high? He didn't quite understand how the image could come from space to the rectangle on the wall. But he trusted the humans of this household and decided to simply take their word for it.

Mel's mom zoomed out to show the continent, zoomed in on what was currently called the United States, and then tightened the focus further to slowly pan toward the southeast. "Follow the water!" Bat exclaimed. "The water leading all the way to the curved shore."

"Here?" Mel asked. "That's . . . Baton Rouge, Louisiana."

"No, no, move in the direction of the rising sun," Bat replied.

"Not Texas or Louisiana," Grampa Halfmoon muttered, consulting his own foldout map retrieved earlier from the truck. "So, from Chicago, we're going south and then east . . . how far?"

"Farther, farther," Bat replied as Mel's finger slid across the screen in response.

"Alabama, possibly Georgia," Ray put in from the sofa.

"By the time we get close, my wing should be healed up enough that I'll be able to fly up to survey the landscape and guide us the rest of the way. This tool is . . ." Bat struggled to find the words. "Useful. Highly impressive. But it's not only the look of the land I navigate by, it's the scents and sounds. The way Wind whispers to my wings."

"Whatever you say," Grampa Halfmoon replied, extending his forearm to Bat. "Kids, you'd best get some shut-eye. We've got a long trip ahead of us."

"Charlie," Mel's mother began. "Have you checked the weather? There's a big winter storm brewing through southern Illinois and Indiana." She suppressed a grin. "You might have to go around it. It's a full day's drive through Iowa City, Des Moines, and Kansas City. I could give my cousins in Kansas a call if you'd like somewhere to stay—"

"Mighty considerate of you," Grampa Halfmoon replied, as if that hadn't been part of his plan all along. "Mighty considerate." He'd wait until after bedding down to text his high school sweetheart, Georgia, and tell her that he'd be passing through town.

In the warm attic, Mel rested her head on her mom's shoulder. They lay side by side on the full-size futon, looking out the window at the cloudy night sky.

"Your dad sends his love," she said, after updating Mel that he'd agreed to her accompanying the Halfmoons on the road trip. "He hopes you have a fun time." Neither of them mentioned that Mel's dad could've texted her that himself. Her mom went on, "I'm sorry I can't come with y'all. I hate how much of my life is eaten up by work." *Hate* wasn't a word that Mel's mother said lightly. She added, "At least I'll have Dragon and Bandit to keep me company while you're gone."

"I thought you loved teaching," Mel replied as Dragon made a show of sharpening her claws on the newly stuffed backpack that rested against the makeshift bookshelf. Mel, who missed her mom and the cat already, had received permission to spring the tabby from the closed-up bathroom for the night on the condition that she texted Grampa Halfmoon, come morning, once the tabby had been safely resecured downstairs. "We should put a tracker on the cat," she said, not entirely kidding. Bat was bunking in Grampa's room, after all, and the last thing they needed was another dustup involving Dragon.

"I do," Mel's mom replied with conviction. "I do love teaching. It's everything that goes with it." She sighed. "Endless meetings, paperwork, and being an adjunct means my position is only guaranteed for six or nine months, renewable. We can't count on it long-term. Plus, I'm an introvert like you. The heavy course load takes a lot out of me." Her brow furrowed. "I'd like to find a position with more job security."

"A position in Chicago?" Mel asked, adjusting the wool blanket.

"Maybe, but I can't make any promises. Grampa Halfmoon has been talking about a move, too. We may not be able to stay here with him and Ray forever."

Mel threaded her fingers through her mom's. They hadn't been living in the bungalow that long—just a few months—but it felt cozy. Mel had her mom, her books, her cat, her new best friend, and even a new grandparent. After all the changes following her parents' split, the Halfmoon bungalow felt like a hug of a home.

Thud. Dragon's assault on the backpack caused it to slip onto the hardwood floor. She fled across the futon, bouncing once on Mel and once on her mother.

"Oof!" Mel's mom exclaimed. Changing to a less fraught subject, she said, "I hope Grampa Halfmoon's reunion with Georgia goes well. After all, *Grandma* Halfmoon is a tough act to follow. You know, she danced in the tradition of Native greats like Maria Tallchief, and then spent a few years fundraising for the ballet company."

"Wow," Mel said with a yawn. "She must've been impressive."

"Yes, and so is Georgia," Mel's mom replied. "Grampa Halfmoon has a type."

6

GRASPING GREED

Saturday morning, it was time to leave on the road trip. Mel's mom hugged her. She hugged Ray and Grampa Halfmoon. Then she hugged Mel again, kissed the top of her head, and whispered, "Melanie Melody, my sweetest song."

Mel's mom picked up a soft food-cooler bag and set it on the floorboard of the back passenger seat of the pickup truck. "I've packed you plenty to eat—baby carrots, celery sticks, granola bars, crackers, apples, oranges, and nuts. There's a jug of fresh water that you can refill—stay hydrated, humans and animals, too!" A week apart sounded like a long time. "Charlie, do you need cash? I've got a couple of fives in my purse. I could run in and—"

"We're almost set," Grampa Halfmoon said, climbing behind the wheel. He dug a GPS out of the central console, attached it to a passenger vent, and plugged the cord into the truck's built-in cigarette lighter. "I know where I'm going. This is just in case there's a hiccup."

Mel's mom let out a long breath. This wasn't her adventure to take, but she could cheer them on from afar and look forward to updates. She called to Bat, "Good luck at the game!"

"Good luck teaching!" he replied from Ray's shoulder.

Ray's backpack, Mel's backpack, and Grampa's weekend roller bag had all been loaded along with the camping duffel, sleeping bags, extra kitchen towels, and fishing gear—including Grampa's lucky fishing hat—into the bed of the truck, and its cover had been closed. Grampa had affixed a #LandBack bumper sticker he'd bought last fall at the annual Chicago powwow. Bat's shoebox had been strapped into the middle of the back seat with bungee cords usually used to secure the patio furniture against storm winds.

As Ray moved to the other side of the truck, the engine sputtered to life, and Gray Squirrel leaped down from the nearest branch, her tiny claws accidentally skimming the top of Mel's long hair before landing on the hood. "Whoa!" Mel exclaimed. "Ow! Squirrel! *Squirrel!*"

Gray Squirrel spat out the nut in her mouth. "Greetings, humans! It is an honor to accompany your party on this grand adventure."

Ray was delighted. "I'm Ray Halfmoon, that's my grandfather, and this is—"

"This isn't Noah's ark," Mel mumbled, adjusting her

beaded hair clip. "I thought talking animals were rare, special, living legends."

Gray Squirrel fluffed her tail. "Perhaps I'm not a legend . . . yet. But any squirrel worth their nuts knows the importance of deciphering human speech." Humans had so much—too much—power. Gray Squirrel considered pointing out that their kind had butchered the hickory tree where she'd nested as a kit. She considered offering thanks to Grampa Halfmoon for always keeping his squirrel feeder filled. Instead, she decided to hold her tiny tongue.

Grampa himself turned up the heater on the dashboard. He took Gray Squirrel's declaration in stride and made a mental note to pick up a variety of nuts and pumpkin seeds before they hit the highway. He'd already been planning to swing by the pet store for mealworms and a few extra cans of wet cat food for Bat and, finally, for a small bag of ice for the cooler when they stopped to fill the gas tank. Those last two tasks would become a morning ritual for the duration of the trip.

"Do you bite?" Mel's mom asked.

Gray Squirrel drew back, paw to her heart, appalled. *"Do you?"*

"Withdrawn." Mel's mom hugged her daughter one last time. "Don't forget to text. Listen to Grampa Halfmoon, and if you need anything—"

"We'll keep in touch," Grampa promised her as everybody else climbed into the back seat. Behind him, seat belts clicked into place. Putting the vehicle into reverse, he glanced at his passengers and said, "Precious cargo."

For most of the cloudy morning, Grampa Halfmoon cruised down I-88 West. He'd decided to leave days earlier than was strictly necessary, for the chance to soak in the sights and visit with folks on the way to their destination. Beyond Chicago, the sky stretched wide, and the land did, too. Our heroes passed by communication towers and power towers, by cows and crop fields dotted with ponds, tractors, and red barns.

As Grampa navigated alongside orange-and-white construction barrels, Gray Squirrel listened to the dance of Wind with the pickup and felt the vibrations of wheels on the highway. She marveled at the countryside and whispered, "I love trees."

Ray reached to gently scratch her head. "Me too."

They traveled over the mighty Mississippi River into the state of Iowa.

A casino resort in Davenport made Mel think of her dad, who often worked weekends, and moments later, a small roadside memorial with a cross reminded her why she hadn't shared her jumble of feelings about him with Ray. At least she still had a dad. And a mom, for that matter, who'd just texted her a selfie with Dragon.

Coming up on a sign for Herbert Hoover National Historic Site, Grampa asked, "You kids want to stop and learn about President Hoover? His vice president was a

Kaw man named Charles Curtis. Depression era—late 1920s, early 1930s."

Truck travel was thrilling! Gray Squirrel could hardly believe how quickly the landscape was whizzing by. But after Grampa Halfmoon had scolded her to stay off the dashboard and out of his line of vision, Gray Squirrel had commandeered the empty car organizer strapped to the back of Grampa's seat. That's normally where Grampa would tuck small purchases and store his prized collection of classic Dolly Parton CDs. To Gray Squirrel, it was dandy—from the center pocket, she could watch Mel and Ray and see out the back and side windows.

Gray Squirrel could hear Bat softly snoring in the shoebox in between the young humans, and, she was pleased to note, the bag of mixed nuts and seeds that Grampa had bought was right on the floorboard beneath Ray's feet. She asked, "What's a president?"

"A leader," Mel said. "Like a principal chief. A vice president is like a second chief." She knew enough about Native-US relations to be cautious of any Native person rising to US federal office back then. Besides, the Great Depression sounded, well, depressing—it was right there in the title. Mel batted the question back to Grampa Halfmoon. "What do you want to do?"

Grampa Halfmoon glanced at the two best friends in the rearview mirror. He believed that young folks deserved to know the truth of history. He thought about saying that people could be complicated. There had been

Native folks of the time who, like Charles Curtis, thought assimilation—leaving their cultures behind—was the only path forward. Grampa strongly disagreed with that notion. He'd also spent much of his life away from his people—in the military and in the city—but he'd always held fast to his tribal identity and traveled to Cherokee Nation as often as he could. "I'd like to stretch my legs, grab a fresh cup of coffee, but there are plenty of other places to stop."

"I'm hungry," Ray said. Never mind that he'd just polished off a granola bar.

Mel suggested, "Hot lunch?"

"Hot lunch it is." Grampa Halfmoon's foot pressed on the accelerator. He'd been concerned about Mel's spirits while she'd been working on her school report about the Trail of Tears. It clearly had weighed on her heart—thoughts of the thousands who'd died, of the survivors ripped from their homelands, the illness and violence they'd suffered. Grampa hoped that the trip would bring Mel comfort and healing. She could wait to learn about Charles Curtis and how his politicking resulted in even more land loss and devastation.

That decided, Grampa took the nearest exit and located a gas station with a spiffy convenience store—a new building designed to look like an old log cabin. A sign in the window read *Homemade Chili and Chicken Noodle Soup!*

"Chili!" the humans exclaimed in unison.

"What's chili?" Gray Squirrel asked.

"Tomatoes and peppers," Ray replied. "Meat and—"

Alarmed, Gray Squirrel sprang from the organizer to the top of Grampa Halfmoon's headrest to peer out the windshield. "*Squirrel* meat?"

"It's okay, it's okay," Mel soothed. "I doubt it's squirrel meat, and if it is, we'll rush right back outside and go somewhere else."

Gray Squirrel pivoted sideways to gauge her sincerity. "You promise?"

"We promise," all three humans said in unison.

Once Grampa turned off the engine, Mel and Ray exited opposite sides of the back seat, and Gray Squirrel began racing around inside the vehicle. "I'm in your seat!" she exclaimed to Ray. "I'm in your seat!" she exclaimed to Mel. "I'm in your seat!" she exclaimed to Grampa. Much as she'd been trying to project maturity and dignity, Gray Squirrel couldn't help herself.

"You go on outside and do your business," Grampa Halfmoon told her. It was another way of saying, "My truck isn't your toilet." He added, "I'll leave the window open enough for you to slip back in. We may be a while." After all, humans had business to do, too.

Inside the store, the bell rang over the entrance. The clerk, Lexie, greeted the incoming kids. Through the front window, she could see the older man they'd arrived with washing the windshield of his pickup truck and that a white, off-road minivan was pulling into the parking lot.

It reassured Lexie, who'd clocked years of babysitting in high school, that her young customers were in the company of a responsible-looking grown-up.

Normally, Lexie wasn't left in charge of the store alone, but her coworker had called in sick at the last moment and the manager was running late from a dentist's appointment. Lexie was a college student in her early twenties, and she liked the part-time job mostly because the owner didn't care if she studied at the counter. She checked the monitor screen for the camera mounted at the top right-hand corner of the room and watched the kids extract a couple of bottles of cold water from a store fridge before returning her attention to her geography textbook.

In addition to food, drinks, motor oil, and miscellaneous items—travel-size toiletries, over-the-counter medicines, magazines—the shop featured inexpensive souvenirs and household decor. Ray always enjoyed perusing stores with a wide array of unexpected items. In Chicago, for example, he loved visiting Murphy Family Antiques. During summers in Oklahoma, he often joined Wilhelmina and his other aunties at garage sales and estate sales.

As Mel tried on sunglasses, Ray surveyed the shelves. The barbecue sauce, mustard, and cinnamon-roasted nuts looked tasty. The Iowa Hawkeyes gear—rain ponchos, ball caps, T-shirts, scarves, gloves, socks, and mugs— were standard. Next to that, the state souvenirs were more of a mixed bag—postcards, bumper stickers, and snow globes, as well as holiday ornaments and magnets and keychain holders in the shape of the state.

Around the corner, the quality of merchandise took a nosedive. Ray stared at the pseudo-Native ones, including imitation dreamcatchers, garish feathers on elastic headbands, and toy tomahawks with rubber blades. Mel said, "Yuck."

Ray scanned the sales tags for identifying information. He doubted any Native artists had a role in producing the junk. He backtracked to grab a couple of yellow-and-black ponchos.

"What're you . . . ?" Mel was briefly mystified. Was Ray expecting rain? But his plan became clear when he started rehanging the ponchos, so they covered up the cheap, fake Native goods. As Mel nodded her approval, the bell over the door jingled to announce Grampa Halfmoon's entrance.

In the truck, Bat awoke in the shoebox, feeling groggy, disoriented, and alone. Where had everybody gone? It seemed like only moments ago he was still in Illinois, bobbing his head to an old Willie Nelson song on the radio. "Charlie! Charlie?"

Bat fluttered to the front of the truck—"Mel? Ray?"—and, from there, to the driver's-side window, still left open a crack. "Gray Squirrel, where did you go?"

By then, Mel, Ray, and Grampa Halfmoon were chowing down on chili—beef, not squirrel—and picking out novelty sunglasses. The latter were a splurge, but

Grampa couldn't resist. Mel had chosen purple butterfly-wing-shaped lenses. Ray had gone for the baseball frames, and Grampa Halfmoon had delighted them by picking out glittery red heart-shaped frames for himself.

The humans couldn't hear Bat from inside the store. Gray Squirrel could faintly detect Bat's voice, but what with Wind whistling through the treetops, she couldn't make out what he was saying. However, someone was listening to Bat—the middle-aged white man who'd been driving the white, hefty-looking off-road van that Lexie the store clerk had noticed pulling in earlier. You may know him as . . .

"Midas Buttinsky, coming to you with a Buttinsky Bulletin—where I *butt in* for a good cause. Today we're off I-80 West, outside of Iowa City, Iowa, where it appears that a bat—that's right, *a bat*—is vocalizing in a manner that sounds like human speech."

A full-grown human male, holding up his phone, approached Bat. He smelled like danger. Where were Bat's friends? There they were! In the opposite direction, on the other side of the glass front of a rectangular building. Bat's friends hadn't abandoned him—of course they wouldn't—but from inside, they couldn't hear him either. "Gray Squirrel!"

The human kept advancing. "It appears as if the animal is being illegally trafficked."

Scrambling onto the roof of the truck, Bat screeched, "Squirrel! Gray Squirrel!" True, with the big rematch potentially riding on his recovery, Bat had been trying not to fly, but this was an emergency. Extending his wings, Bat began to lift off, and then the world went dark.

"Got it!" exclaimed a higher-pitched voice. "Midas, did you—"

"As you all just witnessed," Midas Buttinsky began, as if talking to an audience, "my assistant, Truly, has successfully rescued the animal, and now we must escape before we're detected." His tone shifted then. "Truly, did you pay for the gas?"

"Don't I always pay?" she retorted. "And I'm not your assistant! I'm your sister!"

Screeching for help, Bat deduced that he was inside a cloth drawstring bag. The sister, Truly, swung it without care. Bat went still so as not to exacerbate his wing injury. Who were these wretched humans? What did they want with him?

Perhaps you're wondering, where was Gray Squirrel? She'd recognized the sound of her name and bounded from tree limb to tree limb, skittering across the roof of the convenience store just in time to hear the closing van door cut off Bat's shrieks. Quickly assessing the situation, Gray Squirrel pounded on the shop window with tiny fists, chittering as if hawks were circling.

"What's with that squirrel?" Lexie the clerk asked, drawing her customers' attention.

Mel ran out the door. "Gray Squirrel, what's wrong?" Ray and Grampa Halfmoon followed, and Gray Squirrel rushed down a gutter, reporting what she'd witnessed.

"You kids go back inside," Grampa Halfmoon said. Ray and Mel did not go back inside, but they did keep their distance. Gray Squirrel sprinted toward them. "You there!" Grampa strode toward the van. "What're you doing with that bat?"

Sensing a viral moment, Midas began video-recording the encounter. "Us?" he replied. "We're rescuing it. What were *you* doing with that bat?"

"Be careful with him!" Mel hollered. "Bat is hurt."

"Then it should be at a wildlife rehabilitation center," Midas replied. "You were in possession of a wild animal. A poor, injured wild animal! Do you have a permit for it?"

"Do *you*?" Ray countered. "Bat is our friend. Give him back!"

Suddenly poised for battle on top of Ray's shoulder, Gray Squirrel shrieked.

Another man might've deduced that he looked somehow less serious or intimidating in red sparkly heart sunglasses, but Grampa Halfmoon pushed them up on his nose like he meant business. "Listen, you hooligans—"

"No, you listen, you old coot," Midas said, forgetting for a moment that he was recording.

"No, you *all* listen!" Lexie exclaimed from the shop doorway. "Everybody, calm down, get in your respective vehicles, and leave the property or I'm calling the cops." The clerk had no intention of calling the police, but she didn't want a ruckus in the parking lot. Besides, there were kids involved—the same kids Lexie had silently cheered on as she watched them creatively neutralize the tacky, offensive product display the store manager had installed over her objections. Lexie's inner babysitter had risen up within her, and she resolved that Mel and Ray wouldn't get hurt on her watch but figured she'd have more clout by pretending to be a neutral third party, speaking for the store. Nobody else realized she was bluffing about calling the police, and none of them wanted to deal with law enforcement, questions about permits, or delays either.

"You heard her," Midas said into the phone microphone. "As someone who *butts in* for good causes, I face threats from the establishment every day. Truly, get in the van!" He turned toward his sister. "No, wait, give me that." He roughly grabbed the top of the bohemian-style drawstring purse from his sister and held it so his viewers could see. "Don't y'all worry. Now that I've saved this poor creature from those exotic animal traders, I'm going to nurse it back to health in consultation with qualified local wildlife rehabilitation professionals."

"I said, get in your respective vehicles and leave now." Lexie pointed. "First the van. You go east. Then the pickup. You go west. *Now*, or I'm calling the police."

"We can't let them take Bat!" Mel insisted as they returned to the pickup.

"Easy, sweet girl," Grampa Halfmoon said. "We're not done with those two yet."

Kuk-kuk-kuk-kuk! Gray Squirrel barked furiously. *They would rue the day!*

"The Buttinsky Bulletin," Ray read aloud from the vinyl logo on the side of the minivan as Midas and Truly drove off with Bat.

Great-Grandfather Bat, *the* Bat, had been snatched from his friends, delayed on his very important journey, and so violently jostled in the cloth bag that his muscles ached. He was being held prisoner in a human vehicle without any idea of where it was going. But it smelled like raw ambition and deep-fry grease. Bat could only hope his capture hadn't further aggravated his wing injury. He'd been systematically testing the inside of the bag in hopes of finding a way to escape; however, the drawstrings had been cinched tight and knotted from the outside. If only Bat had the jaws of Gray Squirrel! Then he could have chewed his way out.

"I'm telling you," Midas said. "The bat was talking—like a person talking. Speaking English! I could make out what it was saying. It was calling to that old coot and his kids."

"That is ridiculous," Truly answered. "Your imagination is working on overdrive."

"I know how it sounds, but I heard it with my own ears."

They'd been bickering nonstop for several minutes. From what Bat could tell, Midas was driving, and Truly was doing something in the back of the van. Upon climbing into the driver's seat, Midas had casually tossed the drawstring purse containing Bat behind him, but Truly retrieved it and set it on a smooth, flat surface. She said, "What with the cloud cover, the video lighting could be better. If you—"

"I had to seize the moment," Midas countered. "Too bad that checkout girl threatened to call the cops. The old coot was getting riled up. Could've been clickbait gold, but we've got something even better. That bat is no ordinary contraband. It could make us a fortune."

"The Buttinsky Bulletin is supposed to make us a fortune," Truly grumbled. Raising her voice, she added, "We have fewer subscribers than most house-cat accounts."

"Cats are the toughest competition on the internet," Midas reminded her. "Besides, we haven't been at it that long. It takes time to build an audience. We could save a ton of money on this trip if we slept in the van."

"*I* need a shower. *I* despise public toilets! *I*—"

"Enough yammering, we're already doing it your way. I'm turning into the driveway for the bed-and-breakfast now. That little bat—"

"This little bat is a vile, disgusting rodent—a rat with wings." Truly slid the drawstring purse farther from the sound of her voice. "I'm editing the teaser now. I say we drive it straight to the local wildlife center, get some B-roll there, and move on."

Midas pulled the van onto a crunchy-sounding surface.

"You're the one who wanted to charge into a firehouse in Chicago and order them to paint their trucks green."

"Lime green," she countered with a click. "It's easier to see when—"

He snorted loudly, turned off the engine, and opened his door. "They didn't take kindly to me barging in, hollering about it."

"Which made for top-notch video," Truly pointed out. "Hits went through the roof."

"Be that as it may, now it's *my* turn to decide what we're doing, and my decision is made." Huddled in the dark pouch, Bat couldn't know what passed between the two nefarious human siblings, but he could sense the tension between them simmering in the stale air.

The front door slammed shut again. "Fine, I'm not unreasonable," Midas said, starting the minivan again. "We can swing by the wildlife center, but that's only the beginning. The last thing we're going to do is turn in the bat. Truly, I swear on Daddy's memory—that so-called rat with wings is our golden ticket!"

7

HINTS OF HOPE

Riding in the pickup down the access road, Gray Squirrel muttered, "This is my fault. If only I hadn't left Bat alone!" She scurried across the top of the dashboard, chittering to herself, sitting up now and then to scan the landscape. "My fault, my fault, my fault!"

If only for safety's sake, Grampa Halfmoon would've told her to ride in the vehicle organizer strapped to the back of his seat, but he didn't have the heart to scold her right then. Fortunately, traffic was light to nonexistent. He drove about thirty miles an hour, hoping Gray Squirrel's frenetic activity would help burn off her guilt and stress.

Ray leaned forward. "Gray Squirrel, if you hadn't warned us, we might never have known what happened. Now we've got a better chance of rescuing Bat."

"The Buttinskys couldn't have gone far yet," Mel

observed. "Grampa, what if we jump on the highway and turn around at the first—"

"These bat-nappers could be dangerous," Grampa Halfmoon replied. "We've got a name, *Buttinsky*. Because it's rare, that's more useful than *Smith* or *Johnson*. Probably a stage name to fit their little internet song and dance." He grimaced at the thought. "Anyway, it should be enough to track them. How about I drop off you three off at—"

"*No!*" Ray, Mel, and Gray Squirrel shouted at the same time. To say that none of them had ever pushed back against an Elder so loudly or adamantly was an understatement.

"We can help find them," Ray insisted. "The Buttinskys have Texas plates, not Iowa. They could be staying at a hotel somewhere around here."

That was a good point. Grampa Halfmoon had served as an army mechanic. He had faith in his ability to figure things out. Besides, the kids were right. They could help. So could Gray Squirrel. All of them had committed to taking Bat to the traditional playing field. That put all of them chin-deep in this predicament. Grampa pulled into the lot of a fast-food chicken restaurant located between a fast-food hamburger restaurant and a fast-food taco restaurant. "Let's put our minds to the matter, talk out the problem together."

The wisdom in Grampa's voice reassured Gray Squirrel. Once the truck was parked, she stretched out on the dashboard. The sun had come out that afternoon and, now that she'd begun to calm down, it felt soothing against her fur.

"It looked like the dude was using his phone to record," Mel said from the back seat. Using the web search app on her phone, she added, "Content creators are always posting new videos. They've got to keep the hits coming." Her thumbs were flying. "Here, I found it! The Buttinsky Bulletin. The landing page for their web TV show, social media links, everything."

As Gray Squirrel hopped, hopped, hopped to perch behind her shoulder and study the screen, Mel skimmed the bios. "Midas and Truly Buttinsky. They've already posted twice today, three times yesterday. Nothing on Bat yet. Nothing since we saw them."

Mel shared the link to the Buttinsky Bulletin with Ray's and Grampa Halfmoon's phones. From the episode titles of the web show, it was easy to glean that Midas and Truly were doing a cross-country road trip, announcing each stop on their journey, and video-recording their adventures. Their hook was boldly inserting themselves into other people's business.

Midas Buttinsky had butted in at a public library in Maine by grabbing a book he considered "a classic" and reading it loudly enough to drown out the children's librarian at story time. He had butted into a romantic proposal on top of the Empire State Building to lecture the young couple on marriage. In Lititz, Pennsylvania, he butted in behind a local diner cook's counter to demonstrate "the proper way" to whisk yolks to make scrambled eggs. In Ohio, Midas had taken it upon himself to "fix" the signage of *A Friend in Knead Bakery* to read *A Friend in Need Bakery*. In Indiana, he'd stopped by the side of the road to "rescue" a sedan stuck in the snow, and the car ended up rolling into a steep ditch. Yesterday, in Chicago, a soaking-wet Midas had been tossed out of a city fire station. *Bad call*, Mel thought, bookmarking that video—*In Hot Water*—to watch later and find out why. Chicagoans took the threat of fire *very* seriously. Teaser videos were regularly posted between the longer episodes.

"What's the point?" Ray asked.

"They're causin' conflict," Grampa Halfmoon explained. "Folks are more likely to click a video of a dustup than a video of somebody doin' the everyday work to make the world better." He didn't spend much time on social media, but he paid attention to news stories about how viewers interacted on the internet. "There's such a thing as good trouble, but this isn't it. Like you said, Melanie, it's about clicks. Views. The more they get, the more money they make. That's what they're all about."

"I'd rather watch videos about ferrets . . . and squirrels," Ray put in, prompting Gray Squirrel to fluff up. Ray was considerate that way. He didn't want her to feel left out of the conversation, even though the ways of the internet were a mystery to her.

"The latest location tag is for Prairie Heritage Bed-and-Breakfast!" Mel announced. "It's on a teaser, saying they've arrived in Iowa City."

Grampa turned the engine back on. "Address?" Ray did a quick search and read it aloud as his grandfather keyed it into the GPS.

Mel refreshed her phone screen. "There's a new upload!" She clicked play.

"Buckle up for the Buttinsky Bulletin!" Midas announced over footage of him in a montage of past episodes, punctuated by a clip of Grampa Halfmoon in the gas station parking lot with the scrawl-font label *Illegal Exotic Animal Dealer.* The screen flashed red over Grampa's face, making him look feral and furious. "I'm Midas Buttinsky—butting in for a good cause. If you haven't gotten around to it already, go ahead and click the dollar-sign icon to subscribe and find out how I've rescued an injured bat from the illicit wildlife trade."

Mel frowned. "They're saying that we're selling wild animals."

"No way!" Ray exclaimed. "How can they tell lies like that?"

"Simmer down, kids," Grampa Halfmoon said. "We've got more important things to worry about than that nonsense. What matters is that we have a strong lead on Great-Grandfather Bat's whereabouts. He's countin' on us to rescue him."

From its towering trees to its red-brick roads and historic homes with picket fences, Iowa City was the kind of town where everyone felt welcome. On the way to Prairie

Heritage Bed-and-Breakfast, Mel texted her mom that they were in Iowa and then she and Ray watched a couple of Buttinsky's videos. Each opened with the Buttinsky Bulletin logo, in which the words formed the shape of a butt, and a voice-over. The recordings looked amateurish, with disjointed angles and lots of jump cuts, clearly chosen to amplify the sense of intensity.

Grampa Halfmoon, who was listening from the front seat, said, "By staying on the move—one city one day, the next city the other, they're quickly leavin' any consequences of their actions behind. That run-in with Chicago Fire . . . I figure, if he hadn't been tossed out of the station, Buttinsky could've ended up in city jail for that."

Mel scanned the dates of the posts. "Sometimes they stay in one place for a couple of days. It'll take them time to edit the video they took outside the gas station."

Grampa Halfmoon didn't like the idea of a video of Ray and Mel showing up on the internet, and he suspected Mel's mother wouldn't be happy about it either. But from what he could tell, Midas's camera lens had stayed focused on Grampa.

Wouldn't you know it! Our heroes missed catching the Buttinskys at the historic B and B by less than five minutes. Grampa Halfmoon had used GPS to drive right to it, but the white off-road minivan was nowhere in sight. "Maybe they moved on," he said, cruising by. "Or they're not back yet." Grampa circled the block and wove through the manicured neighborhood, passing under tree branches. He had the truck windows down, and they could hear wind chimes in the distance. Ray noticed laundry hanging from a backyard clothesline. Mel noticed a black cat snoozing on a gently sloped roof.

Upon arriving at an expansive city park that they'd seen earlier, Grampa Halfmoon pulled the truck over and frowned at the web show on his phone. "They seem to be generally heading east-west, so Nebraska?" The Buttinskys' road trip was, after all, part of the concept for their internet series. From episode to episode, viewers could catch up on their latest adventures as they traveled across the country. Iowa was in the middle of the United States—surrounded by Illinois, Wisconsin, Minnesota, South Dakota, Nebraska, and Missouri. So many options, so many directions to choose from. But the web series had launched in Maine, so they certainly seemed to be heading west. Grampa glanced at Gray Squirrel. "How 'bout you take a look around?"

She leaped out Ray's window to the ground and scampered across the grass in the direction of a small collection of green playground equipment. Then she pivoted, rushing back. "You won't go away? You'll be safe?"

Grampa Halfmoon's smile was gentle. "We won't leave without you. We'll be safe."

With that, off she went again. Trailing after her to the play area, Ray took one swing and Mel took the other. Grampa retrieved his billfold from the center console and changed back from his regular eyeglasses—for driving—to his new sunglasses before leaving the truck. In fact, all three were sporting their new sunglasses. The trio looked excellent.

It was a pretty park, Grampa Halfmoon thought, with plenty of trees, a basketball court, picnic tables, a wooden gazebo, and old-timey streetlamps. A nice day, too—nearly 60 degrees. Everything had been going so well before the Buttinskys butted in. The scoundrels!

Sitting on a swing next to Ray, Mel pushed off the ground, which was blanketed in wood mulch, to build momentum. "Midas Buttinsky mentioned *wildlife rehabilitation* twice. You think he was sincere about that?"

"I'm not sure he's sincere about much of anything," Grampa Halfmoon said.

Having relieved herself, Gray Squirrel ran up one side of the support bars for the swing set and down the other, addressing them from upside down. "Everybody safe? Should I keep watch? I'm brilliant at keeping watch! Stupendous! If I'd been keeping watch last time, Bat—"

"Why don't you keep watch?" Grampa Halfmoon said. "Good idea. Wado."

Ray did a quick search and found a list of local licensed rehabilitators and a wildlife center. "Bat's wing is nearly healed. A center would release him after a few days."

"Unless they tried to figure out what type of bat he is," Grampa pointed out, adding another thing to worry about to his list. Bat bore a resemblance to what you might call a Mexican free-tailed bat, but he wasn't exactly typical of any bat species.

Swinging forward, Mel called, "Nebraska fits the Buttinskys' travel pattern. We could get on the highway, drive west, and wait for them to upload a new video. That would cut down on their head start."

With his high-tops, Ray kicked the wood chips on the ground. "I wish there was a way we could know if they've checked out of the bed-and-breakfast."

"We have to be careful," Mel said, swinging backward. "We don't want Midas and Truly to figure out we're looking for them."

"We could use some help." Grampa Halfmoon snapped his fingers. "Jonah graduated from Iowa!" Jonah and Nancy Lee were a young married couple, Menominee-Polish and Choctaw respectively, and friends of the Halfmoons from the American Indian Center of Chicago. "Maybe he knows somebody around here who can give us a hand."

"You could text him," Mel suggested, slowing her flight.

"I'll give him a call," Grampa Halfmoon replied, strolling toward the gazebo for privacy. To his way of thinking, a request for assistance merited an honest-to-goodness voice conversation.

"Hey, Uncle Charlie!" came the answer. Jonah and Nancy Lee had recently moved into a new apartment, and Jonah was in the middle of swapping out a basic showerhead for a rain shower one. But when an Elder calls, you answer. "How're you and Ray doing?"

It took Grampa Halfmoon a while to get around to his request. First, he told Jonah about Mel and her mother moving into the bungalow attic. He and Jonah talked about the Cubs. Then Grampa explained that the youngsters were out of school for the next week due to spring break, and they were all taking a road trip. "Right now, we're at a nice urban park in Iowa City."

"Iowa is my alma mater!" Jonah exclaimed, even though Grampa Halfmoon already knew that. Jonah couldn't help himself. He was a proud Hawkeye.

"You happen to know anyone who'd do an old man a favor—no questions asked?"

"Does it involve hiding bodies?" Jonah joked.

"That's a question," Grampa replied.

"Fair enough." Jonah had been active in NASA (Native American Students Association) during college, but most of the students he'd known well had already graduated. "There was this Meskwaki freshman I met last spring— Zuzu Nelson. Something tells me that she'd be glad to lend a hand."

"Sounds good," Grampa Halfmoon replied, which calmed any concerns Jonah might've had about the Elder's predicament. First off, even though the old-timers claimed Charlie had been a bit wily in his youth, he'd matured into the cautious sort. Losing a son and daughter-in-law to a twister, then his wife to a respiratory disease—tragedies like those had a profound effect on a person. Second, Grampa's sense of responsibility extended beyond Ray and Mel to young folks in general, especially Native ones. In an Indigenous way, Grampa Halfmoon was considered a beloved uncle and grandfather to many in the Chicago intertribal community.

Jonah listened carefully to Grampa so he could pass on the instructions to Zuzu. The more that Grampa Halfmoon talked, the more curious Jonah got.

Maybe the Elder was still wily after all.

≍ 8 ≍

TRAPPED

To keep up his spirits, Ray decorated Great-Grandfather Bat's shoebox. He drew portraits of Bat on both sides— remarkable likenesses. On the lid, working around the air holes, Ray lettered the words: *Property of Bat.*

Watching every stroke of the colored pencils, Gray Squirrel was fascinated. "You're making something out of nothing. Like magic!"

Ray shook his head. "Nope, not out of nothing. The pencil and cardboard are made from trees." He frowned at the tip. "The color comes from wax, I think."

"Could be oil or resin," Grampa Halfmoon said. "Resin is from plants, too."

Trees? Gray Squirrel admired Ray's artwork. She herself used twigs, leaves—yes, *trees*, to build her nests. She liked how her new human friends had given credit to trees for their contribution. It heartened her that they weren't the type to simply take from the natural world without care and consideration. Unlike those nefarious Buttinskys!

Grampa Halfmoon put in, "Ray, the Creator blessed you with a heap of talent, but all your practice has really paid off. It's been a pleasure to watch you grow into it."

"You're such a good artist," Mel agreed. "Bat will love this." The tea towel that had originally lined his box had been regularly changed, but with Grampa's permission, Mel dug through his roller bag for another, fresh one. She decided on terry cloth instead of embroidered cotton. It was less elegant, but cozier. Upon touching the soft material, the words burst out of her. "I'm worried! I'm worried about Bat."

"Well, of course you are," Grampa Halfmoon said, opening his arms to embrace her and then Ray in a hug. "We're all worried."

Gray Squirrel blinked at the distraught humans, who fretted so much about a small Animal. It touched her deeply, especially being a small Animal herself.

Within an hour, a teenager—almost a woman—with dark hair tucked beneath a plain black ball cap showed up at the park on a moped. She was wearing a heavy long-sleeved, button-down white shirt, black pants, and plain black sneakers and had a canvas messenger bag slung across her torso and resting against her back.

As she got off and strode closer, our heroes could make out *Bernice* on her name tag. "I'm Zuzu." Everyone exchanged greetings, except Gray Squirrel, who was frolicking on the ground within hearing distance, trying to project *typical squirrel.*

Zuzu relayed that, according to plan, she'd hand-delivered a fan letter for Midas Buttinsky of the Buttinsky Bulletin at the Prairie Heritage Bed-and-Breakfast. "There was a mail drop in the door, but I rang the bell and chatted up the owner. I had her sign a form I designed and everything. Looked legit, you know. Asked her how business was, and she said it always slows down after college-basketball season."

"Was there a white minivan parked outside?" Mel asked.

"Nah, but get this: there are rows of rectangular windows up and down to either side of the B and B front door. So, after the lady closes it, I step over to the left, watching her bend down to slip the envelope under the first door to the right of the foyer. So, I checked the website for the place, took a close look at the photos, and from the window views, I'd say it's the Ironweed Room. This Buttinsky guy you're looking for, that's where he'll be staying tonight."

"You're amazing!" Ray joked. "Are you some kind of Meskwaki secret agent?"

Suddenly, Zuzu got serious. "You got me there." She slowly shook her head. "The rumors are true. Any form of malfeasance inflicted on Indigenous people and—boom!" She clapped loudly. Ray flinched and Gray

Squirrel shot up to the top of the pavilion. Zuzu added, "We're on it—a highly trained, super sneaky intelligence network of Meskwaki spies."

"For real?" Ray asked.

"Nah, little man," Zuzu replied. "I'm messing with you."

"Ray is a sincere person," Mel said, trying not to smile.

"Good-natured teasin' never hurt anybody." Grampa Halfmoon patted Ray's shoulder. "Nothin' wrong with an earnest soul either." Grampa beamed at the teenage girl. "Zuzu, we're grateful for your sly, sneaky ways!"

That evening, in the Ironweed Room at the Prairie Heritage B and B, Midas Buttinsky held a wire-mesh colander, swiped from a kitchen cabinet, at an angle over the drawstring bag containing Bat. "You think it's hungry?" Midas asked. "It's worth a lot of money. We don't want it to croak before we can cash in."

"Cash in on what?" Truly replied, tying the belt of one of the thick white terry-cloth robes she'd found in the tall wardrobe. "Guano fertilizer? This is ridiculous."

"I'm telling you—it can talk," Buttinsky insisted. "I'm about to prove it."

"Talk or not, you owe me a new purse. I bought that one in Chicago. I didn't even have a chance to use it." She crossed the hardwood floors with the hem of the robe trailing slightly behind her. It was the details like that—fresh robes, complimentary bottles of water, mints on the pillows—that separated the good-enough places from the classy ones.

Exasperated, Truly untied the cord around the top of the bag. Here they were, *on her dime*, in a beautiful, historical Queen Anne home with gorgeous stained glass and woodwork. She wanted to enjoy her stay, but all her younger brother cared about was the disgusting vermin. Truly scolded, "Lift up that colander more. I can barely move my hands."

"We don't want it to escape!" Midas declared. "Don't open the top of the bag too wide. Bats can squeeze through tiny spaces. That's how they get in attics."

Truly shuddered and met his gaze. "Ready?" Midas nodded, and she said, "Now!"

Quick as a wink, she retreated her hands. *Clack* sounded ring of the metal colander on the polished wood, scratching the surface.

"Come out, little bat!" Midas called. "Come out, come out, and say *howdy*!"

Bat did not want to come out and say *howdy*. Bat was hungry. Bat was frustrated and frightened. Make no mistake, he'd been in tough scrapes before. But he'd never felt as alone and vulnerable as he did with these two— what had Charlie Halfmoon called them?—hooligans.

"Come out, little bat!" Midas called again.

Bat closed his eyes and summoned up every shred of hope left in his tiny body. That wasn't much to work with, but he crawled to the top of the purse and stuck his head out.

"There it is!" Midas exclaimed.

"Hush," Truly said. "You'll scare it."

This house had higher ceilings than the Halfmoon roost. The pink-and-lavender roses rising from the nearby vase bore no scent, and the flat white roses on the walls were made of paper. The walnut-wood wardrobe, the white lace curtains, the heavy crown molding . . . Bat kept identifying potential hiding spots. Unfortunately, the round metal cage surrounding him appeared unrelenting, and his captors were staring right at him.

In a quieter voice, Midas asked, "Could you talk for us?"

Bat was not about to give the human the satisfaction. Bat didn't even come all the way out of the bag. The cloth offered a small measure of protection and made him feel less exposed.

Midas cajoled, "Come on, you ugly thing! My pride is on the line."

It should be noted that Bat was considered quite the looker, not only by fellow bats but by all living creatures who appreciated the deeper meaning of beauty. Truly— already bored—took a moment to read the fan letter that had been delivered while she and her brother were out. It was short, perfunctory. *Welcome to Iowa City! Signed, A Fan.*

It surprised and flattered her that someone had tracked

them to the B and B from their social media. Maybe Midas had a point. Maybe they would build an audience over time. He sure had a knack for drama, and the internet fed on that. "It's just a dumb animal."

That was a hateful, awful thing to say, but Bat still held his tongue.

She added, "It's late. I'm taking the bed. You can have the chaise longue—"

"It *talks*!" Midas insisted as the grandfather clock in the foyer chimed in the background. "I swear on Daddy's grave, it speaks English."

Their father's dying wish had been that Truly look after Midas, and she'd been doing her level best. Not only was she funding this road trip to launch their web series, she'd edited video and acted as backup when he'd taken off—video recording—to cause a ruckus at a public library, skyscraper deck, diner kitchen, bakery storefront, roadside accident, and firehouse without much of a plan. Truly exclaimed, "I don't appreciate your invoking Daddy's name!"

"You're jealous because I was his favorite."

Truth was, their father had been disappointed in Midas, and, for that matter, their mother had been, too. They'd named their baby son after an ancient king whose touch, according to legend, could turn anything into gold. They'd chosen the name in hopes that he'd become a grand business success. But after a series of failed money-making schemes, Truly had been named their solo heir on the express condition that she'd support her brother, Midas, in one last venture to make it big, while holding the purse strings. The siblings' parents had both passed away within the past couple of years. Not that they'd let on, but Truly and Midas were still struggling with the loss. The weight of their parents' expectations held them back as much as it pushed them forward, and their grief spilled out in sniping as much as sadness.

Bracing against the cherrywood chest where he'd positioned the cloth bag and metal colander, Midas leaned in closer to Bat, the tip of his nose touching the top of the metal kitchen basket. "I'm not a patient man, little bat. Talk!" Bat ducked his head back inside the bag. "That's it!" Midas seized the bag and retied it, sending Bat tumbling. "Talk or I'll call a pest service. No, I'll toss you in a dumpster. Or a microwave. Talk or else!"

The downstairs window to the Ironweed Room had gone dark what, to Gray Squirrel, felt like forever ago. Prairie Heritage Bed-and-Breakfast had been built in 1893, which was one thing Gray Squirrel had going for her. No matter how well maintained, older homes had settled into their landscapes. Their quirks and imperfections were praised as *charm* or *character* and their ongoing need for repairs was part and parcel of the commitment that they demanded of their caretakers. Gray Squirrel zeroed in on a ripped shingle in the roof over a bay window of the Queen Anne house. The shingle tasted like cedar.

Stately, sinewy, high in fiber. She made short work of gnawing it loose enough to wiggle through.

Grampa Halfmoon had been concerned that a resident of the sleepy neighborhood might become suspicious of an unfamiliar older man and two kids parked so late and so long on a residential street. His plan was simple: Grampa, Ray, and Mel would go to a special midnight showing of the 1977 *Star Wars* in the nearby downtown district. Gray Squirrel would wait until Midas and Truly went to sleep to sneak into the B and B, locate and free Bat, and then both animals would escape the historic house without the bat-nappers being the wiser. Finally, our heroes would meet up at the neighborhood park and vamoose. It was a good plan. Gray Squirrel had assured them that she was confident in her role. None of what went wrong after that could be fairly considered their fault.

In her upstairs suite, Prairie Heritage B and B owner Mrs. Sallow was a pinched but pleasant enough woman with a forced smile who was ill suited to her profession. The retired chef had chosen the innkeeper's life because of its slow pace and the fact that most of her guests didn't require much from her. They were in town to visit friends or family or on business with the local university. Beyond small talk upon check-in and while serving up a mouth-watering breakfast, she had plenty of time to herself for gardening, antiquing, baking, and watching her shows.

Beneath the mosquito netting canopy, Mrs. Sallow rested

on a queen-size bed pillow propped against the mahogany headboard. She'd already turned off the light on her nightstand and put in her earphones to watch a scary TV show on her phone, so as not to disturb the guests staying downstairs. Mrs. Sallow had a love-hate relationship with being afraid. She relished it on the screen, but not in real life.

Because of the earbuds, Mrs. Sallow didn't hear Gray Squirrel scurrying across the roof or gnawing her way through the loose shingle. Mrs. Sallow didn't glance up from the phone screen when a certain squirrel poked her head through the ceiling to look around.

Gray Squirrel sprang from the window trim to the crown molding, a gorgeous leap with excellent form, but confounded by the flickering light of the phone screen, playing shadowy games across the intricately carved and polished dark wood, she'd misjudged the distance. Her tiny claws strained desperately, failing to find purchase. She spread out her body to slow her fall.

Right then, a fearsome ghostly figure suddenly filled Mrs. Sallow's phone screen, as Gray Squirrel plopped onto the canopy netting. Nose to nose, Mrs. Sallow screamed and Gray Squirrel screamed, too! Mrs. Sallow flailed at the canopy and tossed back the ruffled rose-print bedspread, knocking a small basket of potpourri off the nightstand. Gray Squirrel made a break for the foot of the bed, eyeing the open transom window above the door.

* * *

Downstairs, in the Ironweed Room bed, Truly dreamed of sipping a fruity drink and reading a romance novel while lying on a tropical beach. On the chaise longue, her brother, Midas, dreamed of spinning in place, staring up at hundred-dollar bills falling from a blue sky.

"Squirrel! Squirrel! Squirrel!" Mrs. Sallow hollered, thundering down the stairs.

The Buttinskys jolted awake. Midas reached for the handheld camera, always eager for a video opportunity. Truly groaned, rubbed her eyelids, and fumbled for the thick terry-cloth robe she'd draped across the foot of the bed. As the siblings hurried out of the room to investigate, Mrs. Sallow was scanning the ceiling, walls, and floor of the foyer.

"Keep an eye on it!" she ordered her guests. "I'll fetch my broom!"

"On what?" Truly called as the host bustled down the hall to the kitchen.

"The squirrel!" the B and B owner shouted, only then realizing the late hour and that by waking her guests, she'd potentially end up with a one-star review on the internet. Oh well, it was too late now. "Quick!" Mrs. Sallow told them. "Shut the door before it gets in your room." The way she saw it, outside squirrels were cute. Inside squirrels were destructive gremlins that chewed wiring, shredded insulation, and nibbled on antique furnishings.

Truly yawned, dearly wishing that she'd slept through the whole incident. Midas made a genuine effort to search. He looked around the grandfather clock, scanned the Persian rug, and peered at the legs of the hat stand. "I don't see any squirrel."

Mrs. Sallow rushed back out of the kitchen into the hallway with a flashlight in one hand and a broom in another, eager to evict a squirrel she'd never find.

Truly rolled her neck. "Come on. Let's go back to sleep."

Gray Squirrel didn't weigh much more than a pound. Given their blurry state, neither Buttinsky sibling noticed her clinging to the dragging hem of the terry-cloth robe. When Truly closed the door to the Ironweed Room, the squirrel darted behind an artificial bamboo palm and waited for the two humans to fall back to sleep.

Four times, in equal, ticking intervals, Gray Squirrel and Bat listened in silence to the chiming of the tall box in the foyer. Bat couldn't be certain that the squirrel Mrs. Sallow had been shrieking about was Gray Squirrel. After all, squirrels snuck into houses all the time. Still, he couldn't help being cautiously optimistic. Since his incarceration had begun, Bat had found himself startled, indignant, even frightened. But he'd never lost all hope.

In the antique brass bed, Truly's soft snores ebbed and flowed, steady as a stream. On the red velvet chaise longue, Midas's gruffer snores were interrupted by the occasional snort. Despite the drawstring purse and the colander covering it, Bat was almost positive his senses detected a squirrel in the room.

There! Yes! That was clearly the sound of four paws crossing the hardwood floors, the click of claws against the hardware of the antique trunk beneath the bag. The metal ring of the relocated colander made a soft thud against the leather, and gnawing commenced, slicing through the tightly cinched and tied cord. Gray Squirrel pulled open the bag and found herself nose to nose with Great-Grandfather Bat! It was all she could do not to zigzag with joy.

There was no time to spare. She withdrew so he could crawl out. Bat half scurried, half glided across the room, away from the snoring Buttinskys, past the fireplace and artificial bamboo palm, to slide underneath the door as Gray Squirrel exited out of a transom window.

Clack! The precariously perched colander fell to the hardwood floor, and its clattering roused Truly, the lighter sleeper of the Buttinsky siblings. "What was that?"

Blinking, her brother replied, "What was wha—the bat! It's escaped!"

"Escaped?" Truly echoed, pulling the bedspread to her chin. "You mean that thing is loose in here? I still can't believe you brought that disgusting creature—"

"Don't sass me!" he retorted. "I'm the star of the show!"

"Only as long as I say so. Don't forget—I own the van, the trademark, and the web domain. Plus, I'm better on camera. I'm the one who inherited Mama's good looks and charm."

"How dare you invoke Mama!" Midas exclaimed as

Great-Grandfather Bat and Gray Squirrel slipped out through the mail slot in the front door of Prairie Heritage B and B.

"Thank you, Gray Squirrel!" Bat gushed. "You're my hero!"

If squirrels could blush, she would've. Gray Squirrel wasn't sure how much the Buttinskys' rough handling might've set back Bat's recovery, but she wasn't taking any chances. Gray Squirrel was in peak condition and had adrenaline to spare. "Climb on, let's go!"

Exhausted from his ordeal, Bat wasn't inclined to argue. So, he crawled onto her back, and Gray Squirrel sprinted into the moonlight.

In no time, our heroes were reunited at the neighborhood park they'd visited earlier that day. After initial greetings, Bat was eager to return to his shoebox to rest and recover. "Delightful!" he said, touched by Ray's drawings. "Wado, young friend. Thank you!"

The rescue had gone off without a hitch . . . until a police car pulled up behind their truck. An officer, carrying a flashlight, got out of the black squad car and approached the pickup. Grampa checked the rearview mirror and spotted the young white man with light brown hair.

"Take cover," Grampa Halfmoon said, lowering the driver's-side window. Bat scrambled behind the bag of nuts and pumpkin seeds. Gray Squirrel leaped to the top of the cooler and scurried under the front passenger seat, and both Ray and Mel scrunched down in the back. "Not you two kids," Grampa added. "It's probably a neighborhood watch call. Put your hands where he can see 'em. Sit up straight and, unless he asks you a direct question, let me do the talkin'."

After introductions and a check of Grampa Halfmoon's driver's license, the officer asked, "Did you know this park closes at ten p.m.?"

Grampa had boots in his closet older than the officer. "No, sir. I did not."

The flashlight lingered on the Elder's braid. "You're quite a distance from Chicago. What're you doing in Iowa City, out here with these kids in the middle of the night?"

Grampa's hands rested lightly on the steering wheel like it was no big deal. "My grandkids are out of school for spring break, and we're takin' a leisurely road trip. We just saw the original *Star Wars* downtown—the midnight movie. We'd all normally be in bed right now, but it's a holiday for them." He nodded at the GPS attached to the vent. "I was lookin' for a nice place to stay tonight, but that confounded machine sent us off on a wild-goose chase. I figured I'd pull over here and check my paper map that's in the glove compartment."

"Old-school," the officer said, his shoulders relaxing. Sounding more curious than official, the officer added, "Your bumper sticker says, 'Land back.'"

"Yes, sir," Grampa replied, even though it wasn't a question.

The officer had deduced that this was a Native American family. The University of Iowa powwow had been that day, so he assumed that's what had drawn them to town. "You been drinking?" he asked. "Doing drugs?"

"No, sir." Grampa replied. "Never touch the stuff. Don't suppose you could recommend a nice, clean family motel?"

"Hang on." The flashlight shined at Ray's face, then Mel's. Then came the last question: "How did Luke, Leia, Han, and Chewie escape from the garbage compactor on the Death Star?"

"R2-D2," they replied, and that did the trick. The officer gave Grampa directions to a nearby motel. But rather than spending the night in Iowa City, Grampa Halfmoon circled onto the highway, taking a short detour to order a hot cup of coffee from a fast-food drive-through. "I'm going to put some miles between us and the Buttinskys. We'll find a place to stay in Coralville and ask for a late checkout."

⊰ 9 ⊱

UNEXPECTED ENCOUNTER

Like a lot of old trucks, Grampa Halfmoon's pickup coughed now and then, but shortly after turning off I-80 West to get onto I-35 South in West Des Moines, Mel asked, "What was that?"

"Sounded like . . . a congested gurgle," Grampa Halfmoon replied. "Not a good sign, but we'll be at your cousins' place in Kansas soon enough, and we can get it checked out there."

Ray was drawing pictures to offer as gifts, and on top of the front passenger seat, Gray Squirrel posed this way and that, honored to be his chosen model. "This is surprised squirrel!" She crouched on her haunches, front legs dangling, jaw wide open. "This is splooting squirrel!" She flopped on her belly, limbs splayed. "This is superhero squirrel!" She leaned forward onto her left paw with the right one cocked up behind her and tried to look fierce.

Mel laughed. "How do you know about superheroes?"

Gray Squirrel tilted her head, baffled by the question. Wasn't this entire journey in support of a superhero—the legendary Great-Grandfather Bat?

Bat settled himself in the shoebox. His torn wing was no worse for the wear, but his muscles were still aching. In no time, he was snoozing again.

Traffic was light, what with it being a Sunday. Grampa drove past more cows and crop fields, past huge metal windmills and spiffy vintage cars—one on the road and one on a trailer being towed. As they traveled south, the rolling plains slowly transformed into proper hills. Beyond the Missouri state line, he lowered the windows. The day might've been cloudy, but it was a comfy 76 degrees. Mel tapped Ray's wrist and pointed out her window at two horses, one blond and one chestnut. Gray Squirrel stared at a soaring vulture, who had no clue that the famed Bat was nearby. She felt honored and only slightly smug about being in on such an important secret.

Mel used her phone to take a photo of herself holding up a baby carrot and texted it to her mother. Then she continued reading her fantasy novel by Swampy Cree author David A. Robertson. Ray was snacking on celery and switching back and forth between *The Handy Pocket Guide to Bats* from the school library and keying questions into the search engine on his phone. "Today there aren't any reservations in Missouri, but several tribes have lived here. The Quapaw, the Osage, the Kickapoo, the Shawnee—"

"The Cherokee went through Missouri during removal," Mel said, recalling the reading she did for her classroom presentation.

Still searching for information on his phone, Ray took that in. He'd never thought of himself as a history buff like Grampa, and, though he genuinely enjoyed Mrs. Flores's assignments, the subject didn't call to him like it did to Mel. But they were talking about their ancestors, a tragedy that had changed so much for their peoples. "There's a Trail of Tears State Park to the southeast of St. Louis. We're coming up on Wallace State Park soon."

Gray Squirrel, who was snacking on pumpkin seeds, was staring out the windows, thunderstruck by the density of the trees—both leafy and prickly. She had trouble following young humans' conversation, but it sounded serious and thoughtful and like it wasn't her place to pepper them with questions. Gray Squirrel could be excitable and curious, but she was also respectful and considerate.

"Anyone else feelin' peckish?" Grampa asked.

"Me!" Mel and Ray both called from the back seat. Snacks aside, they'd skipped breakfast, eager to get on the road after sleeping in that morning.

Before long, Grampa Halfmoon had stopped at Daisy's Country Diner in Cameron, Missouri, for food and restroom breaks. It was one of those locally owned places with a gumball machine in the entry, "best of" award certificates hanging above the checkout desk along with framed photos of local high school athletes, and a veteran's discount at the register.

Outside, Great-Grandfather Bat slept on in his shoe-box, and Gray Squirrel stayed in the truck to protect him.

The diner was still serving the after-church crowd. Grampa Halfmoon was happy to be in a small town where lunch was more affordable. He, Ray, and Mel split an order of sliders and two baskets of crinkle fries. Water for the kids, sweet tea for the Elder.

"Tastes good," Ray said, after swallowing his first bite.

"So good," Mel agreed, after trying the sandwich. "Bovine deliciousness."

Behind the kitchen pass-through, a Black man wiped his brow. He was about Grampa Halfmoon's age—maybe younger. "Glad you approve!"

Afterward, Grampa tried to start the truck, which made that congested gurgle sound again and went quiet. Again, he tried to no avail. "I'm going to call around to repair shops."

Grampa got out of the truck, made himself comfort-able on a wooden bench in front of the diner, and spent the next forty-five minutes or so finding out that the local options were either pricey or closed on Sundays. Ray fin-ished his drawings for Mel's cousins. Mel texted her mom a photo of him but didn't mention the truck problem. She thought about texting her dad but decided against it. By then, the dining room had mostly emptied out.

A bell over the restaurant door jingled, and the cook came outside. "Need a hand?"

"Truck won't start," Grampa replied, scratching his beard. "I've been callin' around for a tow, but . . . well, I'm on a budget."

"You might try Little Mac's Auto Body Shop," the cook suggested. "It's new in town, and the owner is encouraging satisfied customers to leave good reviews on the internet."

"Says here it's closed Sundays," Grampa said. "You know somethin' I don't?"

"You might say that. I'm Mac Woods—Big Mac—like the burger, only the ones I make are twice as juicy." Big Mac pulled a phone out of his back pocket. He gestured with his thumb to the white lady at the register. "Daisy is my missus. Little Mac's our oldest son."

Turned out that Mac Woods, Junior—Little Mac—was glad to tow the pickup to his auto-body shop and at the family discount, no less. He didn't normally work Sundays. His wife was a minister's daughter who wouldn't hear of it. No more than a peek under the hood until Monday morning, she'd insisted. But Little Mac had pointed out how the Lord wouldn't object to him at least giving an old man and his grandkids a ride. "We compromised," Little Mac explained.

"That's the key to a good marriage," Grampa Halfmoon said. "That and listenin'."

The overnight delay didn't bother Grampa in the slightest. He'd packed his camping and fishing gear for such an occasion and, on the way to the shop, had called to ask about reserving a camping spot at the nearby state park. It was the tail end of the off-season, and Grampa had wondered whether he'd have to pay for both weekend nights. But the camp host who answered the phone said they were welcome to stay and pay for just one night so long as they didn't set up at their site until that evening. Grampa Halfmoon couldn't have been more pleased. In the meantime, Mel and Ray could spend the day fishing in the glorious outdoors.

"I'll jump on this job first thing tomorrow," Little Mac said, pushing Grampa's pickup into the garage. "After I drop off you boondockers, I've got to get back home to the wife and kids. Our girls turn five this week, and we've got a birthday party to plan."

"Twins?" Grampa Halfmoon asked, opening the cover of the pickup bed. At Little Mac's nod, he added, "What a blessing! We have a birthday in our family this week, too."

Mel and Ray transferred the roller bag, the backpacks, and the folded duffel containing the pop-up tent to the back seat of the tow truck. Mel took out her crossbody bag from a zipper compartment and put it on so Gray Squirrel could hide inside. Bat had insisted he'd be fine without the shoebox for a night and crawled into the front pocket of Ray's hoodie.

"We couldn't be more grateful for your kindness," Grampa Halfmoon said.

Little Mac's Auto Body Shop was in a spruced-up old red-brick building with a two-car garage and a small office to one side. The garage door, office door, and trim had been painted white. The lighted sign across the top of the roof and the awning were a royal blue. Grampa said, "Place looks real nice."

"I appreciate your saying so," said Little Mac, who was still in his church clothes. He hitched a thumb in the direction of the liquor store. "Sorry about the across-the-road neighbors." By that, he was referring to the six-foot-tall, wooden cigar-store Indian beside the entrance. It looked like a mishmash of stereotypical images of plains Native men.

Mel and Ray glanced over and shrugged. At the gas station convenience store outside Iowa City, there had been something they could do about the Hollywood Indian merchandise. But they couldn't fight every battle without wearing themselves out. That said, Ray was pondering the novelty signs in the window of the Speedy Market next to the wooden figure—*Bigfoot Crossing, Caution: Men Cooking*, and *Gone Fishing Forever.*

"I'm a good cook," Ray grumbled, vaguely insulted.

"Bigfoot," Grampa Halfmoon read aloud at the same time.

"Oh yeah," Little Mac said, peeking under the hood. "I've heard tell of sightings down south outside of Branson." He started poking around the engine. "Campfire stories." Nodding toward the Speedy Mart, Little Mac added, "Anything to make a buck. We've got our UFO believers, too! Takes all kinds, I suppose!"

Grampa Halfmoon decided to keep his opinions about such things to himself. Mel was more concerned about Gray Squirrel, who'd suddenly begun fidgeting in the crossbody bag. She chirped once and Mel covered the cloth with her hand to muffle the sound. "Shh, he might not appreciate a squirrel riding in his tow truck."

Little Mac shut the hood and declared that the thermostat was broken. "No big thing. Won't break the bank either. I'll hop online and order a new one to ship overnight."

At the check station, the park host took one look at the Elder with two kids and said they could drop off their equipment at the campground before going fishing. He showed them the lake on a map and offered a quick lay of the land, adding, "I'll be here until nine o'clock."

After Little Mac wished them well and drove off, Gray Squirrel chirped and began zigzagging around on the dry leaves and large white gravel. "I *was* quiet! Did you hear how quiet I was? I was quiet even though there was a *very strange scent* at the fix-truck place."

"It's called motor oil," Mel informed her. "Cars and trucks, motorcycles—they have smells like people and animals do."

"I know that!" Gray Squirrel replied. "Do you really think I don't know that? Do you have any idea how many squirrel lives have been smushed by your speeding transports?"

"That one!" Bat pointed with his good wing toward a tree. "No, that one over there! See that hole in the trunk? It's big enough for me and Gray Squirrel to curl up for the night." Ray carried Bat to the oak that had met with his approval. Truth was, being the nocturnal sort, Bat expected to be wide awake between sunset and morning. But the sooner he made himself at home, the sooner he could catch up on his daytime slumber.

Grampa Halfmoon was pleased with the campsite, which featured a patch of soft dirt for the pop-up tent, a covered wooden picnic table, a wooden post with a metal hook, and a firepit with a grate for grilling. The soil was moist but not muddy, as the storm that had struck southern Illinois the day before had only skated by northern Missouri.

Mel, on the other hand, was not thrilled with the situation. Ray and Grampa liked to fish and camp. Her entire family liked to fish and camp. But Mel was the exception. She liked a clean motel, and she loved a fancy hotel. Last summer, when her cousin got married, Mel had stayed with the bridesmaids at the Odawa casino hotel. The year before that, she'd stayed with her mom at a Native educator conference at the Muscogee resort in Tulsa.

"Let's fish!" Ray called, holding out the extra rod they'd packed for her. Their provisions were already down to three-quarters of a box of crackers and a full box of granola bars. Fortunately, they could hike to the check station to fill up the canteens with drinking water.

"Skoden," Mel muttered, though her heart wasn't in it.

Gray Squirrel sprang into the trees. "I will stay and guard Bat!"

Forcing a good-sport smile, Mel didn't care if it made her an uptight city Native; she'd had a taste of the high life and the Wallace State Park campground wasn't it. Then again, as her fingers curled around the fishing rod, she found herself longing for catfish for dinner, so maybe she wasn't so citified after all.

The catfish was delicious. The restrooms were tolerable, and Mel could look forward to a hot shower at her cousins' house the next day. Grampa Halfmoon had declared there was nothing better than fresh air and fell fast asleep. In her own sleeping bag, on the other side of Ray's, Mel was comforted by the fact that at least they wouldn't freeze. The temperature that night was nearly 60 degrees. Since camping would be a fraction of the cost, she was quietly pleased with herself that she hadn't balked and asked to stay at a motel instead.

On the other hand, they would be sleeping with only polyester and fiberglass between them and the forest. It being a Sunday night during the off-season, there were no other campers. Mel had stayed at the lake in Oklahoma plenty of times. But in her grandparents' cabin. Which had indoor plumbing. And solid walls. Mel tried to distract herself by using her flashlight to read her fantasy novel. Ray could sense Mel's apprehension and stayed awake to keep her company. He'd taken dozens of photos of Bat and Gray Squirrel with his phone and was using them for reference as he drew pictures on a sketch pad. These latest ones would be for Aunt Wilhelmina and Uncle Leonard. He hadn't had any luck getting a Wi-Fi connection, and he'd have to recharge his phone in the truck, come morning.

Mel whispered, "When's the last time Grampa changed the batteries in the flashlights?"

Ray's brow wrinkled. How was he supposed to know? "Why?"

"Because maybe we should turn them off instead of running out the batteries. We might need the light to scare off something."

He tapped his colored pencil on his notepad. "We could buy more batteries tomorrow."

"What about tonight?" she pressed, hugging her book. "What if they go out right when we need them? All because we stayed up goofing around, and then it'll be all our fault."

Ray didn't consider reading or drawing goofing around. "There's nothing to be afraid of. Bat and Gray Squirrel have amazing hearing. They would warn us if—"

Right then, Gray Squirrel's warning barks filled the air. Mel and Ray heard heavy footsteps, cracking twigs, and crunching dried leaves.

"Quick, turn off your flashlight!" Mel whispered. "And your phone."

"You *wanted* the light to scare—"

"I changed my mind. What if the light attracts—"

Ray raised his voice. "Shh!"

A hollow, broad, guttural call echoed through the darkness. It went on a long time—a full minute, maybe two. Then again, and again, and again, and again. A creature would need formidable lungs to make such a noise. Or was it *creatures*—calling to one another?

As if from a distance, Ray and Mel could hear more heavy footfalls—long strides.

"What lives in this forest?" she wanted to know. "Should we wake up Grampa?"

Grampa Halfmoon was a healthy, fit man for his age. But he was also doing all the driving on this very long road trip. Yesterday had been taxing, and he'd want to be rested for his reunion with his high school sweetheart the next day. All the ruckus had briefly roused him, but he drifted back off, soothed by Mel and Ray's chatter, the music of the forest, even the long hooting noises that fondly reminded him of adventures of his youth.

"Not yet," Ray said. "I think they're moving away from us."

"What lives in this forest?" Mel repeated. "What *smells* like that?"

Ray, who had spent a fair piece of his summers in Oklahoma, figured most of the same animals that lived there

121

lived in Missouri. He offered her some educated guesses. "Raccoons, foxes, skunks, weasels, badgers—"

"It sounded bigger than any of those," Mel replied.

"Otters—"

"Do not try to distract me with cuteness," she scolded.

Ray blew out a long breath. "Coyotes, bobcats, bears—"

"Bears?" she echoed. "As in, *bears*?"

"Black bears aren't usually aggressive," Ray countered, hoping it wasn't a mama with cubs, who might worry they were a threat. "They're shy like you. If we don't bother them—"

"You think I'm shy?" she asked. Only seconds before, Mel had seemed focused on the mystery creature, but she was mighty self-conscious. He wasn't sure how to answer her question.

Ray had never thought of shyness as a bad thing. But Mel could be prickly. He'd noticed that she hadn't made friends easily at school. It wasn't that people didn't like her, but she tended to withdraw when she felt self-conscious, and not everybody knew what to make of that.

Out in the tree, Gray Squirrel had quieted. But there was a faint *knock, knock, knock, knock* noise coming from deeper in the forest. After a moment, Ray said, "It's gone now."

"Are you sure?"

"As sure as I can be without looking." He reached for the tent zipper, and Mel grabbed his wrist to stop him. She was clearly too high-strung to sleep, so Ray decided to change the subject. "Want to tell me about your cousins in Kansas? Since I'm going to meet them tomorrow, I might as well know what I'm in for."

Outside in the oak, Gray Squirrel whispered to Great-Grandfather Bat, "The stinky being is still lurking nearby, and it looks like it could climb a tree."

"My friend, I'm not afraid," said Bat, who'd been hoping to stretch his good wing and wander around the branches to build up his strength. "You don't need to be either."

"But it's huge!" Gray Squirrel twitched her tail. Being a city squirrel, she was aware of the limits of her experience. "It's like a large human, but not a large human. A bear? I've heard of bears, but I've never met one." She did have experience with that scent, though, from earlier that day, at the car-service station.

⚔ 10 ⚔

OVERNIGHT GUESTS

Early afternoon Monday, Grampa Halfmoon hiked the road from the campground to the nearby day-use area of Wallace State Park. There, he waved to the camp host and met up with Little Mac, who'd replaced the thermostat and towed the pickup from town.

Little Mac patted the hood. "She's good to go, but this old girl has clocked over 150,000 miles. You've done a fine job of taking care of her, but trucks aren't built to last forever."

Grampa shook Little Mac's hand. "So many memories in those miles. It'd sure break my heart to let her go."

Back at the campsite, Ray and Mel struggled a few moments before managing to fold the pop-up tent. She glanced up. "What was that you were barking at last night?"

"Motor oil," Gray Squirrel answered from atop the wooden post with the metal hook.

Perplexed by that answer, Mel wandered into the trees on the other side of the covered picnic table and knelt by an imprint in the ground. "Hey, Ray! Check out this track!"

Ray was no wildlife expert, but he figured he knew more about the outdoors than she did. He trotted to her side. "You're sure it's a track?"

"Yes," she insisted, pointing. "There's a toe, and there's another toe. You can make out the curve of a heel here. That's not a paw. Do you think someone was skulking around in the dark? Look, the dried leaves behind this side edge are freshly crushed."

"Skulking," Gray Squirrel echoed, liking the chewiness of the word. "Skulking."

At the familiar sound of an approaching vehicle, Ray glanced over his shoulder. "The leaves have been decomposing all winter. It makes sense—"

"Come on, pups!" Bat called with authority. "Time to pack up. Grampa Halfmoon has returned with the truck. We've got people to see, places to be. The big ball game is only three days away!" Bat tried to sound casual about the schedule. He respected that his human friends had kin to visit, but their trip had already been delayed twice—by both the Buttinskys and the truck breaking down. Sure, they'd embarked on this journey with some flexibility. He and Grampa both preferred to mosey their way through life on their own pace. But now, Bat couldn't afford any more major delays. After all, his fellow players on the Animal team were counting on him—their legendary MVP!

Moments later, in the pickup, Gray Squirrel nibbled on pumpkin seeds and acorns while Bat enjoyed a juicy mealworm. Heading south, Grampa Halfmoon stopped at the first grocery mart off the highway. While Mel ducked into the single restroom, Grampa Halfmoon restocked their provisions with beef jerky, trail mix, a tube container of potato chips, and extra flashlight batteries for Mel's peace of mind. (Again, he wasn't *that* heavy of a sleeper.) Ray ordered a slice of hot pepperoni pizza for each of them from the counter.

"It's tasty," he informed Mel upon her return. "But nothing beats Chicago deep dish."

Moments later, as they drove to the parking lot exit, Bat asked, "Did you hear that?"

"Hear what?" Ray replied.

Clunk. "That clunking noise," Bat replied.

Clunk. "What clunking noise?" Mel asked.

Clunk. "It's coming from the behind-us part of the truck." Gray Squirrel had gathered that she and Bat had better hearing than the humans, but it seemed rude to point it out.

Clunk. "Oh, that's the sound it makes when we ride over speed bumps," Mel explained with great authority. "Nothing to worry about. Probably potholes or our bags bouncing around." In the light of day, it was easier for Mel to dismiss whatever had been outside the tent the night before. She still wasn't sure about the track she'd found—it had appeared more like a footprint than a paw. But they had been camping in a public park after all. Possibly, the print had been created by a camper or hiker who'd left not long before their arrival. It might not have anything at all to do with the guttural calls from last night.

In less than an hour, our heroes had passed through forest and farmland, the city of Liberty, over the soaring cable-stayed bridge across the Missouri River, through the stone-and-steel skyscrapers of Kansas City, Missouri; across the state line to Kansas, and into the middle-class suburb of Overland Park. Mel pretended to watch *Spy Kids* with Bat, Gray Squirrel, and Ray on his phone.

On Mel's shoulder, Gray Squirrel was gripping a half-gnawed pumpkin seed, her whiskers twitching. "This is the best—what do you call it?"

"Movie," Ray offered.

"This is the best movie I've ever seen!" You won't be surprised to hear it was also the only movie Gray Squirrel had ever seen.

Great-Grandfather Bat restrained himself from mentioning that he'd partaken of a glorious range of outdoor cinema on screens from Vegas to New Jersey. About five minutes in, he realized he'd seen the film before and tucked back into the front pocket of Ray's hooded sweatshirt. Again, Mel was only pretending to watch.

She kept thinking about how Ray had called her shy the night before. Mel remembered her mom mentioning in the attic of the Halfmoon bungalow that the two of them were introverts. Was being shy and an introvert the same thing?

Up front, Grampa Halfmoon called, "Donadagohvi, I-35! This is it, kids! We're headin' west on K-10. Mel, we should arrive at your cousins' house in under an hour."

The smile in his voice was contagious. It reminded Mel that Grampa was due to reunite with his high school sweetheart, Georgia, that very evening. As she texted her mom with an update, neither Mel nor Ray mentioned that this brief detour was taking them in the wrong direction from the traditional playing field. Like Bat, they were mindful of the long distance ahead and the short time to travel it. But in the driver's seat, Grampa was beaming with anticipation. No one could deny his longing heart.

It had turned into a sunny spring day. The suburbs had given way to farmland, broken up by the occasional warehouse or corporate office building. In the pickup truck, our heroes rolled along, cool and breezy as you please, with the windows down. The humans were sporting their novelty sunglasses—the ones with the sparkly heart, butterfly, and baseball frames.

After a quick stop in town to refuel, Grampa Halfmoon drove through the merchants' district of Hannesburg, Kansas, turned at a stop sign, and then—with a *clunk, clunk* and a *clunk, clunk*—passed over the old railroad tracks.

Down the hill, a long-established residential neighborhood, including the Berghoff property, came into view.

Though Mel had a *lot* of cousins, only a handful lived in Kansas. But you never would've known it to see the couple of dozen people socializing in the wraparound front and side yard of the old white farmhouse that the historic German town had grown up around.

Leaning forward between the front seats, Mel scanned the milling crowd for Cousin Rain, as well as her big brother, Fynn; his wife, Natalie; and their toddler, Yanni. They were German and Ojibwe on their dad's side, and cousins to Mel through her Muscogee-Cherokee mom.

Addressing Great-Grandfather Bat and Gray Squirrel, Ray said, "I'll leave my window open so you two can slip out later. Try to stay close, so we can always find you." There were plenty of oak and hickory trees to choose from as well as a detached garage.

"You can count on me!" Gray Squirrel hopped from Mel's lap into the vehicle organizer to wait until the crowd thinned. "I will stay by Bat's side. I will guard him and protect him from hawks and owls and human batnappers." With that, she tucked into a furball.

Bat yawned, content for the time being in the shoebox that Ray had so lovingly decorated during his absence. "Charlie," he began, "when you see your prospective mate, be sure to hover and flap around her. That never fails to impress!"

"Have fun, and don't worry about us," Gray Squirrel

piped up. "I've got everything covered." She flexed her front paws. "I can even open the bag of mealworms for Bat."

Grampa Halfmoon shot Ray an alarmed glance, clearly imagining mealworms all over the cab of the pickup. Ray said, "Don't worry about that, Gray Squirrel. I'll take care of it."

On the drive in from Missouri, the Halfmoons and Mel had decided to keep their animal companions on the down-low. It wasn't that they didn't trust Mel's cousins, but rather that the fewer people who knew about Bat, the better. After the run-in with the Buttinskys, nobody was inclined to take any chances.

In the yard, a boisterous black Labrador retriever bounded between the picnic and foldout tables, nearly colliding with a buffet set up with bowls, casserole dishes, and aluminum baking trays. Catching sight of the pickup, Cousin Rain set down a beverage dispenser of iced tea and began weaving through the crowd to meet them. Rain was a high schooler, a photographer, and a poet. She had long, wavy light brown hair and wore a seed-bead necklace.

As the truck proceeded past the gathering to the gravel driveaway on the far end of the property, Mel could already smell the barbecued brisket. It was sweet of her cousins to make a fuss. Mel often felt self-conscious at get-togethers. But this was different.

The Berghoff home was a family touchstone, filled with warm memories. It was a place Mel had visited year after year as she and her mother traveled between Michigan and Oklahoma. It had been longer than usual since Mel's last visit. On the that previous trip, her parents had still been married. Her dad had come along, too. She was tempted to text him a photo, but this was mom's side of the family. Did that make it a bad idea?

Clunk. Grampa Halfmoon's rear truck wheel caught the corner of the curb as he pulled into the gravel drive behind a classic Ford Mustang and an old Volkswagen Beetle convertible.

"Glad you finally made it!" Rain beamed at Mel, Grampa Halfmoon, and Ray. "Welcome! We've got plenty to eat and lots of people eager to see you."

After Mel made introductions, Fynn and Natalie fetched Mel's and Ray's backpacks from the bed of the pickup. "Leave that roller bag be," Grampa told them. "I can take it."

Fynn, who was tall and broad shouldered, could've hauled in all three bags by himself and tossed Ray over his shoulder, too. But instead, he offered a deferential nod to Grampa.

Mel's truck window was on the side farthest from the house and bordered by overgrown shrubs and a chain-link fence. Ray made sure it was left halfway open, unfastened the bungee cords securing Bat's shoebox, and scooted it toward the door on his side for an easy exit. "How's that?"

"Very considerate," Great-Grandfather Bat replied. "See you tomorrow!"

"Sure you can only stay one night?" Cousin Rain was asking Mel. "I've got school tomorrow, but you could chill out here with Fynn and Yanni until I get home." Rain's sister-in-law, Natalie, worked in town as an editor at the local newspaper. Rain's big brother, Fynn, ran a social media and web design business out of the apartment over the detached garage.

"I wish," Mel replied. "But we're expected at the Cherokee rez tomorrow night. Ray's favorite auntie is turning fifty, so we can't miss that!"

Cousin Rain's hand flew to cover her mouth. "You have a favorite auntie, Ray?" she joked. "Do the rest of your aunties know about this?"

"Mel!" a voice exclaimed. A curvy girl with curly, long dark hair enveloped Mel in a huge hug and swung her in a circle. Another cousin, Ray figured. Across the lawn, a couple of teens were using giant wands and liquid soap to create bubbles that shimmered—lime green and burgundy, sky blue and deep purple—in the afternoon sunshine. Grown-ups played horseshoes and little kids bounced on a netted trampoline.

"Nice set of teeth you've got there," an uncle told Ray, which seemed odd and a little disturbing until somebody mentioned he was a dentist.

"Why don't you come home with us tonight?" an auntie

asked Grampa Halfmoon, patting his shoulder. "Let the kids cut loose here. Rain can look after them."

Cheerfully taking in the chaos, Grampa replied, "That's a mighty nice offer. As a matter of fact, I'd be happy to take y'all up on it."

"No trouble at all," the uncle said, "and it'll be a lot quieter at our place."

Mel gave a *Good Medicine* journal to Rain, and a bundle of picture books by Kim Rogers of Wichita and Affiliated Tribes to Fynn and Natalie for their daughter. Ray presented his new drawings to Mel's cousins.

"This squirrel looks like a big personality!" Rain exclaimed.

You have no idea, Ray thought. He excused himself to go inside and change from his sweatshirt hoodie to a T-shirt. That also gave him a chance to wander through the rest of the gathering. Grampa's Halfmoon's high school sweetheart, Georgia, was nowhere to be found.

As Sun blurred in cloudy streaks of orange, gold, and fuchsia, Mel texted her mother a series of photos from the afternoon picnic and swayed—with her sneakers kicked off—next to Cousin Rain, who was wearing what had been Grampa Halfmoon's heart-shaped sunglasses, on the creaky porch swing. Mel had always looked up to Rain, who was five years older. While the girls caught up, Ray was playing fetch with Chewie, the resident black Lab, in the yard.

Gray Squirrel, who was watching them, would regularly leap from her hidey-hole with Bat to a higher branch to survey the scene for any threats. She'd already gone on a barking jag about a silver tabby atop the across-the-street neighbor's new horizontal wood fence. "Cat! Cat! Cat! Cat!" Periodically, she'd send out a reminder. "Kuk-kuk-kuk-kuk!" Neither Gray Squirrel nor Great-Grandfather Bat had forgotten their perilous encounter with Dragon.

As Ray tossed the ball for the dog again, Cousin Rain called, "Hey, city boy! What do you think of Hannesburg, Kansas?"

On the drive through town, Ray had seen houses with peeling paint and sheets for curtains next to dolled-up ones that looked like stops on a tour of historic homes. There were more American flags than he was used to. The downtown district had been carefully restored. People waved and smiled as they passed by. The picnic dishes were delicious, and the crowd was friendly. "I like it," he replied. "Tiny compared to Chicago. Lots of white people."

"Yeah, mostly German-American—we've got an annual Bierfest and everything." Rain tilted her head at the sound of her niece wailing inside, but then her brother's nurturing voice wafted through, and Rain relaxed again. "My brother even owns lederhosen. But there's a local Indigenous scene, too, what with Haskell Indian Nations University less than half an hour away. Aunt Georgia's summer camp for Native teens has taken off over the past couple of years."

Ray was not impressed. "Your aunt Georgia stood up Grampa. Total no-show today."

"You think he's upset?" Mel asked. She'd noticed, too, of course.

Ray jogged over to the porch with the dog following. "Of course Grampa is upset! You saw how fast he took off after the picnic with your auntie and uncle. You and your mom . . ." He shook his head at Mel as if horrified by them both. "Talk about buttinskys!"

Mel was insulted. "How about we leave my mom out of it? She was just—"

"Whoa!" Rain exclaimed, taken off guard by their intensity. "Nobody stood up anybody. I was over at Aunt Georgia's house yesterday, helping her pick out an outfit for dinner tonight." Rain patted her knees and her dog trotted to her, tail wagging. "Since they were going out for barbecue, she wasn't sure about the embroidered white cardigan. But she loves the sunflowers around the collar, and she could always take it off if—"

"I don't care what she's wearing!" Ray exclaimed, and then caught himself up short. "Sorry, I didn't mean to . . . Let me get this straight. The date is happening—now?"

"Yes," Rain replied. "The date *is* happening. Now."

Delighted, Mel leaned forward, resting her elbow on her knee and her chin in her palm. She hid her widening smile behind her splayed fingers. "And they're going out for barbecue?"

"Yes," Rain replied. "They're at Tricia's Barbecue House. Best beef tips in northeast Kansas. It's a Hannesburg institution. It's—wait, where do you think you're off to?"

Mel was putting on her sneakers. "Where do you think?"

⤚ 11 ⤙

BUTTING IN

Mel knew exactly where she was going. Family dinner at Tricia's Barbecue House had become a tradition for the cousins. It was only about a five-minute walk, near the Phillips 66 gas station where Grampa Halfmoon had stopped earlier. "I have to know how Grampa and Georgia's date is going!" Mel exclaimed. "We'll peek into a window at the restaurant. Find out if they're laughing or holding hands."

"That's spying!" Rain exclaimed. "They've got fifty years to catch up on. Don't you think they deserve some privacy?" Wagging his tail, Chewie tried to gauge whether they were staying home or going for a walk. Walk, he begged silently. Walk, walk, walk, *walk!*

As Mel skipped past Ray to the concrete walkway, he called, "Wait! Where are you going?" He turned to Rain. "She's your cousin. Stop her."

"She's *your* best friend," Rain replied, standing. "You stop her."

Walk, glorious walk! Chewie bounded off the porch, making the executive decision that they'd all follow Mel instead.

Minutes later, outside Tricia's Barbecue House, even the picnic-stuffed humans salivated at the spicy smell of smoking beef. The black Lab, who'd been deprived of any people food—despite long tables of it spread across his territory for much of the afternoon—was drooling.

Mel peered in the front window of the busy restaurant. "Is Georgia's hair still dyed red?"

"Not like it was," her cousin replied. "She's been letting that grow out, but getting red highlights in the new gray, so it's less of a drastic change." Strictly speaking, that was more information than Mel had needed, but being a photographer, Rain was more aware of the nuances of light and color than most people. In any case, Mel couldn't seem to spot the couple.

On Monday nights, Tricia's Barbecue House boasted a hot-wings special that packed in the locals. The dining room was L-shaped, with hardwood floors, matching walls, an oversize bar with a huge mirror behind it, wooden tables, and metal chairs. Colorful vintage-style neon signs advertising everything from cola to petroleum decorated the wood-planked walls. "I don't see Grampa," Ray said. Three little blond boys at the table on the other side of the window were making funny faces at them. Rain put a hand on her younger companions' shoulders and gently pulled them away from the glass. "That's my vice principal's family. If we're going to do this, we should at least try to be more subtle."

"What if we go in and say we need to use the restrooms?" Mel asked.

Ray pointed to a sign in the window saying the facilities were for customers only. "What if we got an order to go?"

"We already have barbecue in the fridge at home," Cousin Rain replied. Her sister-in-law had packaged up a big pan of leftovers from the picnic. "Besides . . ." Rain checked her pockets. "My last paycheck went to camera equipment. With tax and tip, we can afford corn bread, onion rings, or fried mushrooms." As a regular customer, she had the menu memorized.

"I love corn bread," Ray replied.

"How can you possibly still be hungry?" Mel asked him.

Chewie had his front paws on the windowsill and his nose to the glass. *Meat!*

"There's more seating toward the back of the building," Cousin Rain said with a sigh, gesturing for them to follow. She might not have been an Elder, but she was *their* elder, and Rain felt obliged to set a good example. On the other hand, while Mel was family, Ray was a bona fide guest, which made Cousin Rain a host, and she was trying to be a good one.

Beyond that, Rain was likewise tempted by the prospect of a glimpse of the lovebirds, finally reunited. Aunt Georgia had told her the story of how she'd long ago snuck out of her parents' house to meet up with Charlie and how they went to Queen in concert at the fairgrounds arena in Oklahoma City. "My, Charlie was a fine sight to see in those bootcut jeans!" Aunt Georgia had exclaimed, and Rain had laughed, cheerfully scandalized.

With forced casualness, Rain added, "Most of the smaller tables are situated across from the chicken-wings bar, which is definitely getting a workout tonight."

"Wings bar?" Ray echoed. As a Chicagoan, he associated headline barbecue with sausage and ribs, but apparently, Kansans went all out to celebrate a wider array of meat selections.

"You know," Cousin Rain said, turning the corner of the brick building. "Buffalo wings, honey-mustard wings, garlic wings . . ." She gestured toward the parking lot. "That's Aunt Georgia's station wagon."

If anything, the aroma of smoking meat was even stronger outside the rear of the brick building. Chewie whined and pawed at Rain's leg. He was such a good boy! Everyone said so. She often said so. Why was she not rewarding him with scrumptious food? It smelled so good!

"There they are!" exclaimed Mel, ducking under a rear window.

"Where?" Ray asked as she pulled him down beside her.

"Against that far wall, under the neon motorcycle sign," Rain replied.

The couple was seated across from a local business owner, Bernadette Rae, and her best friend, which meant that Aunt Georgia's date was sure to be the topic of the week at Bernadette's Beauty Salon. In fact, Bernadette Rae, a notorious busybody, appeared to have her phone pointed at the Elders, either taking a photo or recording video. Rain was briefly horrified before realizing that she was in no position to judge.

Chewie whined again, and Rain absently scratched behind his ears. "Easy, boy."

Then the exit opened, and Rain's pastor held the door for his wife. Chewie took advantage of the opportunity to dart inside the barbecue-house dining room.

Rain exclaimed, "Chewie, no!"

"Cassidy Rain!" the pastor's wife exclaimed. "What on earth are you doing?"

"Hi there!" Rain replied. "Praise Jesus!" She darted inside. *"Chewie!"* She chased after him with Mel and Ray at her heels. "Chewie, come back!" The Berghoffs were a well-known old-town family. Since Chewie tended to accompany her when she was out and about, and went running with her big brother, pretty much everybody in the dining room knew and liked him, too, and—health code violation or not—they were perfectly happy to indulge him in a little attention, but it was Georgia who exclaimed, "Chewie boy!"

Upon recognizing one of his favorite humans—one who periodically gifted him with delectable venison knucklebones—Chewie sprinted to greet her, lunging to the right of the stainless-steel chicken-wings bar, knocking into a tall waitress carrying a large serving tray on her shoulder. The oval tray had been loaded with two large glasses of sweet iced tea, two small plastic bowls of hickory beans and two of creamy coleslaw, two combo plates of burnt ends, and worst of all, two bowls of extra-hot barbecue sauce.

Upon colliding with the dog, the waitress lost her balance, the plastic tray tipped backward, and in trying to catch it, she accidentally knocked it higher and at a sharp angle.

The heavier items—the beans, coleslaw, plates, cups, and silverware—clattered to the stained concrete floor, making a mess and a ruckus. No real harm done. But the extra barbecue sauce bowls landed right-side up—*smack, smack*—on the Elders' table, splashing their clothes, eyeglasses, hair, and faces.

For a heart-stopping moment, the room went deathly silent, and then Georgia said, "Well, Charlie, how do you like me now—red-hot and *spicy*!"

His burst of laughter reassured their rapt audience that nobody had been harmed in the accident, and the other diners joined in, many applauding. The waitress and service assistants rushed into clean-up mode. Tricia, the owner of the establishment, bustled over to apologize, confirmed no one was hurt, distributed two handfuls of individually packaged wet wipes, and whisked Georgia's white cardigan to the restroom to try to get the sauce out before a stain set.

Cousin Rain, now holding Chewie firmly by the top of his collar, stepped in front of Mel and Ray. "I'm sorry," she said. "This is all my fault. I shouldn't have let them—"

"No harm done," Grampa Halfmoon said, cleaning his beard. "No matter what, this would be a night we'd never forget, but now we've really got a story to tell."

It'll make a hilarious video, too, thought Bernadette Rae as she added a music file to her latest social media post and uploaded it to the internet.

Georgia warmly greeted Cassidy Rain and Mel, who she affectionately called *dear girls.* "I've heard so much about you, Ray Halfmoon." She wiped sauce off her fingers before extending her hand for him to shake. "My goodness, you're the living image of your grandfather!" She winked at her date. "I should go clean up. Excuse me, I'll be right back."

"Take your time," Grampa Halfmoon called. "I'll be doin' the same shortly."

Right off, Ray could see how happy Grampa was with Georgia, and that made Ray happy, too. He asked, "Does this mean we can stay for chicken wings?"

Grampa chuckled. "No, you can't stay for chicken

wings." He grinned up at Rain. "Get these rug rats home and keep 'em out of any further trouble. I've got wooin' to do."

That night, beside her cousin Rain, under a Broken Star quilt, Mel slept more deeply than she had since her parents had divorced. Mel dreamed of beading, even though she wasn't a beader like the local auntie whose King Ranch casserole she'd devoured that day. But Auntie and her mom were there in the dream, and so were both of her grandmothers—the Muscogee one and the Odawa one. So was Rain's mother, who'd passed away years before. Together, they were gathering loose beads in oranges and reds, yellows and greens, to repair a frayed design. It was a restful dream, a sweet dream. Still, she felt a whisper of longing for her dad.

Outside, the sunrise flickered at the edge of Earth. Great-Grandfather Bat exclaimed, "Oh, how I'm loving all this warm spring air!" The farther south they went, the warmer it got. After a long, cold, lonely winter, Bat found the change of seasons and scenery delightful.

Two branches up, Gray Squirrel was determined to express her concerns. "I—I'm not—respectfully, sir, that silver cat was prowling about not so long ago. I lost sight of him at sunset. And I'm almost certain I spotted a hawk circling in the sky above and beyond the house."

"Look again," Bat countered, grooming his fur. "That

isn't a hawk. It's a hawk-shaped kite, a human pup's plaything that got tangled in overhead wires. See how it dangles?"

Gray Squirrel struck her thinker pose. "That's not what I was talking about. Great-Grandfather, I swear it was a hawk—*a bird of prey*—and it was flying behind that wooden pole."

Bat crawled farther onto the branch and craned his neck to gaze up at her. "Gray Squirrel, I appreciate your protecting me on this journey, but—"

"You were bat-napped!" she exclaimed, scaling down the trunk and hopping beside him. "It was my fault. My fault! Mine, mine, mine! I wasn't paying attention."

"That was the doing of those conniving Buttinsky humans, not you. Through your courage and daring, you rescued me from them. Your warning barks may well have saved my life from Dragon, too. But I'm practically healed. Yes, it's important to err on the side of caution. The big game is coming up soon. After tonight, we have only two moonrises to get to the traditional playing field, and then the athletes will gather the following evening. I have every intention of counting myself among them." Due to the preference of some players for day and others for night, it had been agreed that any sporting events that included both Birds and Animals would be planned to commence around dusk.

"What was that?" Gray Squirrel asked, her tail at alert. "Did you hear something?"

Though Bat was feeling smothered by Gray Squirrel's overprotectiveness, and he was pretty sure the gray tabby had moved on, he had too much respect for Gray Squirrel to dismiss her fretting out of hand. Bat listened. He could hear Wind in the trees, the flapping of the kite against the utilities pole, the distant cry of a train whistle, and—yes, he *did* hear something odd for the hour—the *crunch, crunch, crunch, crunch* of footsteps on gravel. "That's not a cat."

Kuk-kuk-kuk-kuk! Gray Squirrel barked at the top of her tiny lungs. Fast asleep in a sleigh bed, Fynn, Natalie, and Yanni couldn't hear her. Under a knitted blanket on the living-room couch, Ray couldn't hear her. Neither could cousins Mel and Rain, but at the foot of Rain's bed, Chewie threw back his head and barked—arf-arf, arf-arf, arf-arf, arf-arf—waking up the whole house. He ran out to the couple's bedroom door. Arf-arf, arf-arf, arf-arf, arf-arf!

Within seconds, overhead lights illuminated the windows and the porches. Fynn quickly checked on everybody and shouted, "Rain, watch the baby!" Natalie ran to peer out the storm door as a shadowy figure tore out from behind Grampa Halfmoon's truck and high-footed it down the street. Fynn, who was a runner, came up behind his wife, and caught a glimpse over her shoulder of the fleeing trespasser. "Should I go after him?"

"And then do what?" Natalie shook her head. "There have been a lot of vehicle break-ins near downtown lately." As part of her job at the *Hannesburg Weekly Examiner*, she studied the local crime reports. "We should've told Charlie to clear any valuables out of his truck."

Up in the tree, Bat asked Gray Squirrel, "Did you get a good look at who it was?"

Gray Squirrel felt torn between the urge to give chase and her responsibility to Bat. "I couldn't see. The interloper was on the far side of the truck. Full-grown human. Probably male."

"I can catch up with him," Bat insisted, positioning himself to take flight.

"No!" Gray Squirrel moaned, catching sight of a more dire thread. "You should rest your wing. Besides, look there! It's Barn Owl!"

After their earlier conversation about the hawk, Bat was skeptical of her warning. But then he saw Barn Owl resting on the roof of the garage apartment. Slowly, cautiously, he and Gray Squirrel retreated deeper into the tree cover.

Fynn jogged over to confirm that Grampa Halfmoon's pickup windows were still intact, the doors were still locked, and the cover of the truck bed was still secure. "There's a rear passenger-side window rolled down," Fynn called. He looked around the property one more time. "We scared off whoever it was. Ask Ray to come check if there's anything missing."

Seconds later, Ray dutifully went outside and confirmed that everything that had been in the cab of the truck was still in the cab of the truck. What Ray didn't notice was the micro GPS tracker that had been slipped beneath the padding and attached to the inside bottom of Bat's shoebox. The shoebox Ray had lovingly decorated and personalized with Bat's name, not realizing that Midas Buttinsky would take advantage of that kindness to zero in on his target.

That's right, that greedy hooligan Midas! He and Truly had stayed at a hotel in Des Moines the night before—planning to butt in at a women's leadership conference the next day—when Midas stumbled across a brand-new, viral video of the old man and his kids on social media. Tricia's Barbecue House had been tagged. Midas had used that information to trace our heroes to the historic northeast Kansas neighborhood and drove around with his sister until he'd spotted Grampa's pickup truck in the Berghoffs' driveaway.

Truly, who'd drifted off in the driver's seat, was startled awake as Midas climbed into the van, parked on a street a few blocks away from the Berghoff house, on a hill near an elementary school. "Did you find the bat?"

Midas buckled his seat belt. "Not yet. They must've taken it inside the house with them. But there's no way they'll get away from us now!" It had taken convincing—smooth talking that dissolved into begging—to convince Truly to sign off on chasing after the bat. But the video from Tricia's Barbecue House wasn't the only one getting a lot of views.

Partly due to breaking celebrity news involving one of

the many actors who'd played Batman, search engine algorithms had pointed a record-breaking number of viewers to the Buttinsky Bulletin teaser featuring the bat, Midas, and the old man in the parking lot outside Iowa City. With their advertising revenue at stake, the Buttinskys wanted nothing more than to deliver the promised full-blown bat episode to their soaring number of subscribers.

⊰ 12 ⊱

BACKWOODS SURPRISE

Come morning, Grampa Halfmoon knocked on the front door just as Mel and Ray were finishing up Natalie's signature sweet potato hash with runny eggs in the Berghoffs' country kitchen. Not long afterward, our heroes offered thanks and bid farewell to Mel's cousins and piled back in the truck. Grampa Halfmoon double-checked his paper foldout map and confirmed the route—59 South through Richmond and Garnett to 169 South through Iola, Cherryvale, and Coffeyville, Kansas, then to the east on US 60 around Nowata, Oklahoma, and south on US 69.

After they'd been on the road awhile, Mel cajoled, "You're really not going to tell us about the date with Georgia?"

Grampa grinned at her in the rearview mirror. "Nope."

"Are you going to see her again?" Ray asked.

"Yep." He was a man of few words where romance was concerned.

They drove by cornfields and water towers, a medical center and cow pastures, railroad tracks and a grain elevator, two steak restaurants and windmills, and a house with a large cross mounted to the road-facing chimney.

Shortly beyond an RV park, Grampa gestured toward the oil refinery in the distance. "Gas is awful expensive, what with how close we are to oil country."

As they went by a flea market, a dozen motorcyclists roared by in ball caps, blue jeans, bandanas, black shades, and black leather vests. Otherwise, the traffic was light.

Not far beyond the Oklahoma state line, they spotted a Cherokee casino, followed by oil pumps, and it struck Mel how the landscape had shifted from farmland to ranchland.

"Gray Squirrel, look!" Ray exclaimed, pointing out his window. "Camels!"

Mel leaned forward to see. "Wow. Cool!"

"Camel? What's a camel?" Gray Squirrel dropped her acorn and sprang from the top of the bag of feed to find out. After the thrills that had been cows and horses, she honestly hadn't expected any animal to top them. But in this case, the humans seemed especially excited.

Gray Squirrel blinked. To her, the pair of camels resembled those other large grazing, hoofed animals, though their backs featured noticeable humps. "Camels live here."

"Not usually," Mel and Ray said at the same time.

Forests rose from wide-open cattle fields. Grampa

Halfmoon smiled at the sight of the red dirt between the rocks on either side of the road. All said and done, it was about four hours door to door from Mel's cousins' home in Kansas to Ray's aunt and uncle's in Cherokee Nation.

Once they arrived at the address, Grampa Halfmoon leaned out of the driver's-side window and punched the call button on the gate box. "Congratulations! It's the lottery."

"Lucky us!" exclaimed Uncle Leonard's voice as the gate swung open.

Clunk. The long, slightly winding asphalt drive was riddled with potholes. *Clunk.* Grampa Halfmoon did his best to steer around them.

Clunk. He said, "Last time I was out here, I lost a hubcap."

Once they reached the house, the Halfmoons and Mel got out of the pickup and Uncle Leonard threw an arm around Ray. "You're getting so big! Why, you are the spitting image of your dad, and you've got your mama's smile, too."

Grampa Halfmoon opened the cover of the truck bed. "Something's been making a racket back here. I heard it clunk on every pothole." He peered in and did a double take. "How on the blessed green earth did this awful thing get in my truck?"

"What is it?" Mel asked, coming around to help carry in the bags. "Oh."

"Oh, what?" Ray asked, reaching for his backpack. *"Oh!"*

Do y'all happen to recall the wooden cigar-store Indian from outside the liquor store across the road from Little Mac's Auto Body Shop in Missouri? It had been slid into the bed of the pickup, all the way toward the front of the vehicle, against the cab. That was what had been making the *clunk* sound. Mel and the Halfmoons hadn't noticed it behind their camping gear. Uncle Leonard yanked out the wooden figure and set it upright on a stepping stone.

Mel frowned, thinking it over. "It must've happened that night when the pickup was at Mac's Auto Body Shop. But Little Mac never would've put this in here."

Grampa Halfmoon rubbed his beard. "Nope, he was upset that it was on the other side of the road from his business. He even apologized to us about it, not that it was his fault. It's not like he could control the across-the-street neighbor."

"Hang on." Uncle Leonard was using the magnifying glass function on his phone. "Look here." He reached under the painted wooden figure and pulled out a tuft of matted hair caught in a crack in the left shoulder. "Hm. This hair doesn't look human to me."

It didn't appear especially inhuman to Ray or Mel. Uncle Leonard tested the texture between his fingers, lifted it to his nose, sniffed, and jerked back slightly. "Hmm." He glanced sideways at Grampa Halfmoon and gestured with his thumb at the cigar-store Indian. "Maybe somebody trusted you to get rid of it."

Grampa Halfmoon ran a finger back and forth under his nose like he was trying to wipe away a grin. "Leonard, let's get the bags inside. Ray, why don't you give Mel a tour of the property? Too bad you're missing Wilhelmina's veggie garden at the height of its glory, but we'll be back again, come summer."

"Speaking of Mina . . ." Uncle Leonard went on to explain that she was in downtown Tahlequah, for a birthday lunch at a Mexican restaurant with friends, but she'd be home for a cozier family celebration that evening. Originally, before the trip delays, Grampa Halfmoon had planned an early celebration of her big birthday. This worked out even better.

Each taking an end, the men hauled the cigar-store Indian to the stack of firewood off to the side of the house and then carried in the bags. Once the front door shut behind them, Ray and Mel introduced Bat and Gray Squirrel to the area. Mel echoed, "Mina?"

"Short for *Wilhelmina*," Ray replied as they strolled by the tire swing and vegetable garden.

Gray Squirrel, who'd been cooped up, was zigzagging down the hill toward the dock. She bounced off trunks and sprang from branch to branch, delighted by the leaf buds of spring, the faint, rising crow of a rooster—even though she didn't know what a rooster was.

"Great-Grandfather Bat," Mel began. "Do *you* know anything about that wooden Indian?" On Ray's shoulder, Bat bobbed his head, and she added, "You going to fill us in?"

Right then, the forest went quiet. Mel and Ray hadn't been paying attention to the rustling of the foliage, the bird cries in the distance. But the silence was loud. Startling. Undeniable. Gray Squirrel hurried to Ray's feet. "Bat, sir, you've been recognized!"

"Bound to happen sooner or later. I'm surprised we managed to get this far without somebody making a fuss." Bat figured the fact that he was in the company of human pups was only adding to the reaction. "Gray Squirrel, could you do me a favor?" Her ears went alert, and her tail rose to attention. Bat went on, "I don't want anyone fretting over me or any rumors to get out of control. Put out an alert that I am traveling with these humans of my own free will, that they are trusted friends." Surveying the wooded landscape, he picked out a home base. "Once Moon is high, I'll welcome community questions from that tree house over there."

A good choice, Ray thought. He had fond memories of that tree house.

Bat added, "If any low-to-the-ground relatives show up, we'll relocate to a lower rung of the ladder leading up to it." It occurred to him that white-tailed deer were common in these parts, and wild hogs were expanding their territory every day. Figuring Ray's local kinsman was a hunter, Bat added, "Tell them to be careful, though, or else they may end up in a stew."

Gray Squirrel could hardly believe her tiny ears. She had been elevated to Great-Grandfather Bat's official spokes-squirrel. "You can count on me!"

Sensing that Great-Grandfather Bat needed to mentally prepare for the night ahead, Mel dropped the subject of the cigar-store Indian. But reflecting on the sounds she'd heard overnight while camping, the partial footprint she'd found at the state park the next morning, and what Little Mac had mentioned about local lore, all signs pointed in the same direction.

Midafternoon, Aunt Wilhelmina bustled in, carrying half a sheet cake covered with chocolate icing and multicolored sprinkles. She was with her best friend, and they made quite the pair—Crystal Jean in metallic silver tennis shoes and matching fingernail polish, and Wilhelmina sporting a necklace of colorful LED letters spelling *Happy Birthday*, a sash that read *Birthday Girl*, and a rhinestone tiara. As greetings filled the rustic living room, they radiated celebratory energy.

"Oh my goodness!" Aunt Wilhelmina exclaimed, putting down the big cardboard cake box. "I didn't realize y'all would beat me home. I do apologize, Melanie! What you must think! Leonard, did you offer these children something to eat? Why aren't they eating anything?"

"Of course not," Uncle Leonard replied. "You know we never feed company."

"That's not funny," she scolded affectionately, giving Grampa Halfmoon and Ray hugs and kisses on the cheeks. "It's nice to have you here, hon," she added, welcoming Mel, before introducing her to Crystal Jean. "I love this woman like a sister. You would not believe the trouble she went to today. All the decorations matched the invitations—the napkins, the flowers, the party favors—everything!" Crystal Jean was the daughter of a Choctaw guy and a white woman from Fort Worth. Together, she and Aunt Wilhelmina had a formidable auntie vibe. "You really shouldn't have," Auntie Wilhelmina said. "But I'm sure glad you did."

"You're worth it!" Crystal Jean insisted, putting an arm around her friend. "Besides, you know me! I do love an occasion."

"Crystal Jean is a wedding planner," Uncle Leonard said.

"And a savvy, successful business owner!" Aunt Wilhelmina clasped her hands. "Enough chitchat! We've got a favor to ask." She addressed Grampa Halfmoon. "By any chance, could Crystal borrow your truck? It's sort of an emergency."

"Sort of how?" Grampa Halfmoon wanted to know. It wasn't like him to hesitate. Grampa was always up for doing a favor for a friend. But Great-Grandfather Bat was counting on him (and that pickup) to reach the traditional playing fields in two days.

Crystal perched on the broad armrest of the recliner where he was sitting. "This high-end event rentals outfit in the Dallas suburbs went belly-up, and turns out, they're unloading party equipment cheap to pay off their debts. We're talking chocolate fountains, dance floors, tables and chairs, fiberglass patio gazebos!" Crystal Jean fanned herself with her hand as if she was about to swoon. "You name it. I could provide all that to my clients myself. This could take my whole operation to the next level. I'd be there already, except of course not even my bountiful affection for table skirting can compete with my love for Wilhelmina."

Personal space, Ray thought. Since when was Grampa Halfmoon getting all this female attention? "It's Oklahoma," he said. "Don't you know anybody with a truck?"

Grampa Halfmoon shot him a warning look, and Ray suspected they'd be having a conversation about that later. But Ray couldn't help himself. They were on a mission for Great-Grandfather Bat. A transportation mission.

"Such a smart boy," Crystal Jean replied, touching Grampa's shoulder. "As a matter of fact, my husband, brother, and brother-in-law are already there. One truck each. But I need to see what's what for myself. We're coming right back tonight. Tomorrow, I've got a ten a.m.

fitting with a bridal party at the boutique downtown."

Grampa Halfmoon dug into his jeans pocket and handed the key fob to Crystal Jean. "All I ask is that you have her back in one piece, gassed up and ready to go, by sunrise. Me and the kids, we've got to get back on the highway."

After Crystal Jean thanked him and hopped up, Grampa said to Ray and Mel, "You two run out to the truck and clean it up." They took that to mean they should clear out the bags of squirrel food and mealworms. There wasn't much of it left, so they simply gathered the loose plastic up top, knotted it, and hauled it with the cooler to the tree house. Figuring Bat wouldn't need his shoebox until the next day, they left that on the floorboard in the back seat.

The Buttinskys spent that same Tuesday on the road, following Grampa Halfmoon's truck but trying not to look like they were following Grampa Halfmoon's truck. By the time they neared the vaguest vicinity of Aunt Wilhelmina and Uncle Leonard's place, Crystal Jean was already cruising south down 69 to meet up with her family at the party-equipment sale.

Midas had removed magnetic *The Buttinsky Bulletin* logos from the sides of the white off-road van so he and Truly could travel incognito. They were relieved when the tracker let them know that Grampa Halfmoon's pickup had finally stopped for a good long while and followed the signal all the way to the warehouse parking lot in Plano, a suburb of Dallas.

"What is this place?" Truly asked from the front passenger seat.

"Your guess is as good as mine," answered Midas, behind the steering wheel.

"Well, I'm not going to sit here guessing. We've been driving for hours. I need to stretch my legs anyway." Truly got out of the van and weaved through the nearly full parking lot, right up to Grampa Halfmoon's truck, and peered in, shielding either side of her eyes with her hands to block out the glare on the windows. The sun was falling, but it was over 80 degrees.

The shoebox that Midas had described was on the floorboard, the truck doors were locked, the windows were up, and the cab was otherwise empty. A middle-aged brown man with graying hair passed by, pushing two tall silver outdoor space heaters on a hardwood dolly.

Truly said, "Looks like good quality."

He grinned. "I've got a coffee shop in Frisco." Gesturing at the heaters, he added, "Just what I need for my winter patio business. I was lucky to get these two. They went fast."

"Anything good left?" Truly asked, realizing that some kind of sale was going on.

"Nice quality fake plants," he replied, adjusting his ball cap. "Columns and easels, a couple of gazebos, a brass raffle drum. There's a whole bunch of flatware. You can still find plenty of gems in there, if you hurry. They're not closing tonight until eight o'clock."

Midas, who'd been peeved by Truly's attitude, took his sweet time catching up to her. When she told him what she'd found out, he replied, "Why would the old coot come here? More than that, why would he drive halfway across the country to come here? You think he still has his kids with him? It doesn't make any sense."

Truly set a hand on each of her brother's shoulders and looked him in the eye. "It doesn't make any sense for us to be here either. I say we cut our losses and delete the teaser bat video from Iowa, or we could post that the follow-up episode is unavailable due to technical issues."

"Our most popular web teaser in weeks, and no payoff?" Midas replied. "We can't disappoint our followers. I thought we settled this back in Des Moines. We're sticking with this story. We're going to see it through. Did it ever occur to you that I'm trying to make us rich?"

Truly thumped the hood of the truck. "Did it ever occur to you that I don't want to go through the rest of my life being called *Truly Buttinsky*? Our name is Butler."

A parking space opened immediately behind the truck, so she stood between the yellow lines while he fetched the minivan to claim it. Then they resumed bickering until Crystal Jean, her husband, her brother, and her brother-in-law showed up and began loading and strapping down purchases—most notably a gazebo—onto the bed of Grampa Halfmoon's pickup.

In the front seat of the minivan, the Buttinsky siblings exclaimed, "Who are they?"

Truly opened the door to get out. "I'm going to find out."

"Me too," her brother muttered.

"Just so long as you let me do the talking." Seconds later, putting on a bright smile, Truly called, "Howdy!" When Crystal Jean turned around, Truly added, "Oh, my mistake! I could've sworn that truck belonged to a friend of mine." She gestured at the #LandBack bumper sticker. "His even has a sticker exactly like that."

"Hey there," Crystal Jean replied. "Your friend wouldn't happen to be a good-looking older fella named Charlie Halfmoon, would he? If so, you've got the right pickup. He loaned it to me today so I could run this"— she spread her arms wide—"little shopping errand here."

Midas clasped his hands. "Charlie it is!" he exclaimed, ignoring his sister's side-eye appeal to hush up. "Will you be returning the truck to him anytime soon?"

"On my way now," she replied. "Forgive my manners. I'm Crystal Jean. That's my husband, Mark; his brother, Herb; and my brother, Todd." The men offered nods, used to the way Crystal Jean chatted up everyone she met. She went on, "And you are?"

"Uh," Midas began. "She's Tr—"

"Trixie," Truly replied, taking Crystal Jean's hand. "This is Travis."

"Where do y'all know Charlie from?" Crystal Jean asked, making conversation.

After a pause that went on a beat too long, Midas glanced at the license plate. "Illinois!"

"Charlie will be sawing logs by the time we get home to Oklahoma," Crystal Jean said. "And he'll be moving on come morning. Too bad I won't get a chance to tell him that y'all said hey."

❊ 13 ❊

SENDING A MESSAGE

For Aunt Wilhelmina's second birthday party of the day, Uncle Leonard served venison stew from the slow cooker with the leftover grocery-store sheet cake.

Auntie Mina, as Mel had begun to think of her, presented them with hand-knitted scarves. They gave her a beaded hair clip from the annual Chicago powwow, a box of Frango Mint Chocolates, and the purple butterfly sunglasses. Ray also presented his aunt with a portrait of her knitting by the fireplace as well as one of Uncle Leonard wood carving at the dock.

"This is really something, kiddo!" she told Ray, admiring his artwork. "I'm going to pick up picture frames next time I'm out and hang these with the family photos in the hallway."

"You should draw Grampa and his girlfriend, Georgia," Mel said, finishing her cake.

"Georgia?" Uncle Leonard asked as Aunt Wilhelmina exclaimed, "Girlfriend!"

"Don't you think you're getting ahead of yourself?" Grampa Halfmoon took a sip of coffee. "Now I'll never hear the end of it." Not that Grampa seemed to mind telling the story.

After being caught up on Grampa's love life, Uncle Leonard said, "Well, you've been alone for a long time. I'm glad to hear you might've found someone for companionship."

Ray set down his cake fork. Grampa Halfmoon hadn't been alone. He'd been living with Ray for practically Ray's entire life. Georgia seemed like a nice enough person, and Grampa clearly had enjoyed spending time with her. But one of them lived in Kansas and the other one lived in Chicago, so how much companionship could possibly come of that?

"It's not like I'm planning to propose any time soon," Grampa replied, waving them off.

"But you *are* planning to propose eventually?" Mel wanted to know.

"Don't wait too long," Aunt Wilhelmina said before Grampa could reply. "These big birthdays—you know, the years that end with a zero—they make you appreciate how time flies."

Ray had turned ten a couple of years earlier and he hadn't given the 1-0 a second thought, but he knew better than to argue with his Elders.

* * *

Later that evening, Grampa Halfmoon retired to the guest room he'd be sharing with Ray. While Aunt Wilhelmina made the sofa into a bed for Mel, Ray and his uncle went outside.

"I hope you don't mind Wonder Woman sheets," Auntie said. "My girls, they're both big fans. My youngest, she's finishing up at Bacone College." Mel was familiar with the school, located in the city of Muskogee. "Her big sister is a carpenter in Oklahoma City. She does art shows and cabinets—whatever pays the bills. Takes after her dad when it comes to woodwork."

"I'm a Wonder Woman fan, too," Mel assured her, studying the Trail of Tears painting over the fireplace. "That's beautiful," she added. "And sad." It was stylized rather than realistic. An uneven line of ancestors, viewed from behind, trudging through ice and snow. It wasn't the only piece of Cherokee art in the room. Mel noted the baskets to either side of the fireplace.

Auntie Mina said, "If you need anything in the night, we're right down the hall, past the bathroom. You knock or holler and I'll be right there, quick as you please."

Sliding under the covers in her pj's, Mel might've bristled a bit if her mom had fussed over her so much, but something about Auntie Mina doing it felt reassuring. Mel felt comfortable enough to ask, "What's the difference between being shy and being introverted?"

Sensing the weight of the question, Auntie Mina sank onto the far corner of the sofa. "Well, I'm no expert. But take Leonard, for example. I'd say he's introverted. Don't get me wrong. He likes people well enough, especially in small groups like we had tonight. But crowds, they wear him out. Most of the time, he's happy with his own company." She winked. "And mine. *Introverted* is a personality type. *Shy* is something else, though that's not to say a someone can't be both. Why do you ask?"

Mel thought it over. If yesterday's picnic in Kansas had been any indication, she wasn't a total introvert. She'd had fun tonight, and last night had been one of the best of her life. Mel could hardly remember the last time she'd laughed so hard. She'd even been the leader, making the decision to go to the barbecue house. If only she felt as comfortable with the kids at school as she did with her closest friends and family. "I think I'm shy."

Auntie Mina folded her hands in her lap. "Do you fret about what people are thinking of you? Or do you worry about—"

"Making a fool out of myself?" Mel blew out a long breath. "Yeah. It wasn't this bad before my parents split up. I mean, I'm not . . . you know, some damaged kid from a broken family or whatever. It was . . . There was more going on than that."

"I see. May I ask what all happened?"

"First, my dad moved back to his rez, the Odawa rez.

He started over with a new family like it was no big deal. Then my best friend, Emma . . ." No, that wasn't right. "My ex–best friend, Emma—Ray is my best friend now—anyway, she moved to Lansing, and it's like she forgot I'm alive. Then my mom and I moved from Kalamazoo to Chicago to live in Ray and Grampa Halfmoon's attic." Mel paused. "It's a pretty attic. We like it." She didn't want Auntie Mina to think she wasn't grateful or didn't like the Halfmoon bungalow.

"That's a lot of change," Auntie Mina said. "Leonard and I try to take a vacation every summer. We've visited the Rocky Mountains, the Ozarks, even Nashville. But I've lived around here my whole life. Sometimes I wonder if I'm missing out, but home is home, you know?"

Mel couldn't quite relate. These days, the idea of *home* felt more complicated. "At least my dad chose to move out, and Emma's parents chose to move away, and my mom and I chose to move to Chicago." Mel gestured at the Trail of Tears painting. "I mean, our ancestors went through much worse. Compared to all that, I've got nothing to complain about. I mean, I'm not Cherokee, but—"

"Of course, I get your meaning. Your ancestors were removed, too." Auntie Mina absently patted the covers over Mel's feet. "It's true that they suffered. What happened was a terrible wrong. But, sweet girl, that doesn't mean you're not allowed to be a whole person and feel every kind of emotion. What you're talking about . . . family and friendship—feeling like you do or don't belong. That's a lot of what life is made up of. It's not betraying your ancestors or making light of what they had to go through; it's the reason they survived and rebuilt— for their children and their children's children to live full lives. For you."

Outside, Ray normally would've climbed up to the tree house, but since Bat and Gray Squirrel were in there, he got into the tire swing instead. Leaning against the tree trunk, Uncle Leonard said, "I couldn't help noticing that you didn't have much to say about your grandfather's girl-friend. Don't you like her?"

"She's okay, I guess," Ray admitted, pushing off the ground to build momentum. "She sure took it like a champ when my cousin's dog made a huge mess of her hair and outfit."

Uncle reached into his jeans pocket for one of his carv-ing tools and a piece of wood. "I sense a *but* coming."

Ray insisted, "I want Grampa to be happy . . ."

Uncle Leonard raised a knowing eyebrow. "But?"

"But in Chicago, it's mostly been the two of us."

"I see."

For a long while, neither of them said anything. Ray flew back and forth in the tire. Uncle Leonard whittled away at the wood.

Finally, as Ray started to slow, Uncle said, "I've lived hereabouts since the day I was born—except for the years I was in the service. I've been married to Mina for—well, let's just say it's been a while. But, nephew, *change* is the definition of *life*. There's no escaping it."

"What's that supposed to mean?" Ray asked. "The past doesn't matter?"

"Of course it matters!" Uncle's voice went sharp. He put away his carving tool and what looked to be a rough wooden inchworm and reached out with one hand to stop the swinging rope. In a softer tone, he explained. "Ray, this Georgia . . . she's your grampa's past, present, and future. Even if he never spoke to her again, she'd still hold a place in his heart. Like your parents have in your heart and mine. Whether we're together or apart, we still love them."

Ray extracted himself from the center of the tire. "I don't even remember them. My parents, I mean." It felt painful to admit to himself, worse to say the words out loud.

Uncle Leonard pulled Ray into a bear hug. "That's okay. They remember you."

Midas Buttinsky had many qualities, but persistence—or stubbornness, depending on your point of view—was foremost among them. Despite the pushback Truly gave him, he'd always been the baby of the family and tended to get his way. Lacking another destination, Midas had managed to convince his sister to follow the pickup back to Oklahoma. Truly figured that, by now, the old man had probably let the disgusting creature go or had otherwise gotten rid of it. But the bat itself wasn't crucial—she could splice in stock footage of any bat later during production. The plan was that the Buttinskys knock on the front door, proclaim that they were confiscating the bat to bring it to animal rescue, and demand that the old man surrender the animal immediately.

Truly figured either the old man would refuse so Midas could end the episode by warning Buttinsky Bulletin viewers to be on the lookout for the illegal exotic animal traders or the old man would give her brother the disgusting thing and, once she'd gotten plenty of footage, they'd dump it. As for Midas, he still didn't doubt for a minute that he'd heard the bat talking. Just thinking about all the ways he could make money off a talking animal made his head spin.

By the time Moon glowed high, Crystal Jean had returned Grampa Halfmoon's truck, tossed the key fob under the welcome mat, and ridden off with her husband. In the nearby trees, several of Great-Grandfather Bat's fellow bats had gathered. Several of Gray Squirrel's fellow squirrels had gathered. Foxes and deer, raccoons and opossums, rabbits and skunks, coyotes and chipmunks, and snakes and turtles had gathered. No camels, Gray Squirrel noted.

Then a sounder of wild hogs arrived—three sows with impressive tusks and their noisy young. Bat assumed that the mothers had brought them mostly for educational purposes. Birds kept their distance, and Gray Squirrel assumed that was out of respect for the Animals' privacy. But of course, they were aware that there was a meeting going on. Birds know everything.

Gray Squirrel bustled out from the tree house onto a sturdy branch, folded her front paws together, and sat on her haunches. "It's my honor to introduce to you Great-Grandfather Bat, *the* Bat, the one and only. The famed bat that carries the mantle . . ." Her gaze fell to the piglets, and her sense of self-importance fell, too. As Gray Squirrel spoke, she wasn't striking any pose. She was simply being her best, most sincere self. In that moment, it was her message that mattered. "Great-Grandfather Bat is an Elder and a leader of the Animals. We should show him the utmost respect when he speaks." The piglets quieted right away.

"Thank you, Gray Squirrel." Bat crawled out on the branch behind her, and she deferred by leaping to the next closest one. He added, "Welcome, friends. I understand that a lot of you are excited about the upcoming ball game with the Birds in the traditional playing fields." Bat spread his wings, revealing to Gray Squirrel that the tear had completely healed. "Suffice it to say that I look forward to facing off against our rivals, and may the best team win!"

With a hop of glee, Gray Squirrel piped up, "Any questions?"

Fox lifted her snout. "Please forgive me for the interruption, sir. It's an honor to meet you, and I know I speak for everyone hereabouts when we say we're a bit over-whelmed. But I wanted to call everyone's attention to a rising scent, not human, nothing I've ever smelled before, and . . . am I the only one who hears a knocking sound?"

"I hear it," Gray Squirrel chirped, uneasy conversing with Fox, even if no-hunting protocols applied. "I smell it, too." *Motor oil*, she thought.

Then Blue Jay soared into the circle. "My apologies for the intrusion! Two humans—one male, and one female—left their boxy metal migration machine by the side of the nearby road." That description didn't fit Grampa Halfmoon's pickup, and the truck had already been returned anyway. "They're sneaking up on the local human caretakers' nest. They're moving low, close to the ground in an uncharacteristic manner for their bipedal species. Very suspicious."

Bat's thoughts flew to his friends. He'd interpreted Blue Jay to mean that two threatening humans in a van or maybe an SUV were making their way to Uncle Leonard and Aunt Wilhelmina's country house, where the lights were off and everyone was asleep.

What if it was the Buttinskys? They couldn't drive all the way to the front of the house, Bat realized, without using the call box to request that the gate be opened to let their van through. "What color was their machine?" Bat asked. "And the humans, were they adults or juve-niles?"

"The machine was white," confirmed the bird. "Two

adults, and they were making noises at each other. Quiet, but hostile. As if they were about to battle for dominance."

It couldn't be a coincidence that Grampa Halfmoon's vehicle had been targeted the night before in Kansas, and now two trespassers were approaching. "Midas and Truly," Bat said to Gray Squirrel. "I'd bet my furry behind it's them."

"Oh no!" Addressing those assembled, Gray Squirrel said, "We must protect Bat."

"They'll never recapture me here," Bat declared. At the word *capture*, most of the small land animals immediately fled. Craning his head toward Blue Jay, Bat asked, "Are these humans staying near the road?" That would make sense, he thought, if they didn't want to get lost.

At Blue Jay's confirmation, Mother Hog said, "The road isn't far from here, Great-Grandfather Bat. We'll head them off and herd them back to their machine. Watch our young!" With that, Mother Hog, Mom Hog, and Mama Hog left their precious piglets in the other animals' care and rushed through the thick foliage to confront the Buttinskys.

"Try to keep the noise down!" Great-Grandfather Bat called, to no avail. Fortunately, the road was a fair distance from the house, and humans, by nature, were not nocturnal.

Moments later, Truly and Midas began to hear deep growling, squealing, and the sound of shattering twigs and branches, of brush torn to pieces. It was getting louder.

As the forest shuddered, Truly exclaimed, "What's that?"

"Probably livestock," Midas replied. "I'm sure the animals are safely corralled."

"The animals are getting closer," she replied. "They're coming this way!"

Suddenly, three enormous, screaming sows burst from between the trees and brush onto the road and charged Truly and Midas. At the sight of the snouts and terrifying tusks, Truly screamed and dropped her video camera. Midas screamed and dropped his microphone. He shouted, "Run, Truly, run!"

All three furry sows gave their battle cry and chased, chased, chased the Buttinskys away from Uncle Leonard and Aunt Wilhelmina's house to the white minivan parked along the side of the road. The Buttinskys scrambled to open, shut, and lock the doors. Midas punched the start button, steered the van around, and floored the accelerator. Clutching the dashboard, Truly checked her side mirror. "They're still after us!"

The sure-footed hogs galloped after the rolling white box. They gave chase, side by side, throwing their heads back and bellowing. They could've easily run down the humans, but the goal was simply to scare them off. It was a glorious night! Mother Hog, Mom Hog, and Mama Hog had not only met a living legend in Great-Grandfather Bat, they also had been given his blessing to fully embrace their feral nature and target these pesky human troublemakers. In the storied and distinguished history of hogdom, never before had three matriarchs had so much fun.

What's that? Y'all figuring that's the last time those Buttinskys would dare try to butt in with our heroes? Not so fast! Truly and Midas had invested in days of driving, wasted a fair share of time on the round trip to Texas, lost valuable equipment, and sacrificed their dignity. Whatever it took, they wouldn't give up now.

⤜ 14 ⤝

TRACKING SYSTEM

The following morning, Ray awoke to the sound of an axe splitting wood. He slipped out from beneath the Cherokee Seven Clans quilt that had wrapped him cozy and safe and hurried toward the smell of Aunt Wilhelmina's crackle-fried bacon. In a gesture that had made Mel homesick for her mom, Auntie Mina had already packed a going-away care package full of BLTs, PB&Js, bananas, apples, raisins, raw pecans, and whole-grain chips. Uncle Leonard had begun carving a new, smaller figure from the wood that used to be the cigar-store Indian. *Upcycling*, he called it.

Once Mel and Ray finished waving goodbye through the rear truck window, Bat peeked out from Ray's pocket and Gray Squirrel popped up from the vehicle organizer on the back of Grampa Halfmoon's seat. Gray Squirrel exclaimed, "They were here! No, not quite *here*, but on their way here! To the truck, to the human nest where you were sleeping! The mother hogs handled everything. The hogs were *awe-some*! And the baby hogs were adorable! So, so cute! Never call them *swine*. That's offensive. But *boar* is perfectly acceptable. Mom Hog even prefers it." Gray Squirrel had learned so much about other animals on this trip.

"What?" Ray replied. "Slow down, Gray Squirrel. What are you talking about?"

"The Buttinskys," Bat announced with gravity as he perched atop the front passenger seat. "They tried to sneak up on your kin's roost last night. A trio of hogs chased them off."

"How did they find out where we were?" Mel's hand flew to her mouth. "The man who tried to break into Grampa's truck in Kansas! What if that was Midas?"

"Seems like we would've noticed them followin' us all this way." Grampa Halfmoon checked his rearview and side mirrors. He kept his voice calm and steady as he took inventory of the situation. "Y'all keep your eyes open. Bat, how is your wing?"

"All healed up!" Great-Grandfather Bat declared with confidence. "And I've gotten plenty of exercise around the tear to strengthen my muscles. I'll be as ready as ever to play ball tomorrow evening." Strictly speaking, he no longer needed his travel shoebox now that his wing was less vulnerable. But it might still be useful for hiding, and Bat adored it for sentimental reasons.

"That's too far for you to fly," Grampa muttered, ruling out the possibility of getting Bat to safety by separating and sending him on his way. "You'd wear yourself out by the time you got to the playing field, and that would defeat the whole point." In a louder voice, he said, "We can't know for sure what these Buttinskys are capable of. Kids, we're goin' to swing around and head to Tulsa." Grampa Halfmoon had briefly considered returning Ray and Mel to Aunt Wilhelmina and Uncle Leonard's house, but then how would the kids get back to Illinois in time for school the following Monday? "I'm puttin' you two on a nonstop flight to Chicago—"

"You can't!" Ray exclaimed. "I mean, Bat is counting on *all* of us take him to the game." Gray Squirrel and Bat hunkered down where they were. This was a human family dispute, and they felt like they should stay out of it.

"We've come this far," Mel argued, her thumbs flying on the tiny keyboard. She noticed that Cousin Rain had texted her the previous night, but Mel had more pressing matters to deal with. "Last-minute plane tickets"—she held up her phone screen, though Grampa Halfmoon kept his eyes on the road—"might as well be a hundred million dollars!"

Grampa Halfmoon was on a tight budget, but Ray and Mel's safety was priceless. Grampa was moved, though, by how seriously the youngsters took their responsibility to Great-Grandfather Bat. It came from a deep, loving place that couldn't be lightly dismissed.

"You might need our help," Mel pointed out. "I know, we're kids. But Gray Squirrel is even littler than we are, and she rescued Bat from the Buttinskys at the B and B."

"Single-handedly!" Ray added. "I mean, single-*pawedly*."

Gray Squirrel was beaming quietly, in a humble way. Or as humble as she could muster.

With reluctance, Great-Grandfather Bat piped up. "Charlie, old friend," he began. "I understand and respect your instinct to protect the youngsters. At the same time, Mel's ancestors were caretakers of the traditional playing field. Walking in their footsteps could help heal the tear in her heart."

In the rearview mirror, Grampa Halfmoon saw Mel's eyes mist up and Ray put a comforting hand over hers. For a long moment, everyone was quiet. Mel thought about how she'd felt since reflecting deeply on the Trail of Tears for her school report. She thought about what it meant for a descendant of survivors to have the chance to return home.

Home. What it meant had felt so uncertain, so change-able. But what if it wasn't? What if her true home—or at least the first and forever home among a few—was wait-ing ahead?

Great-Grandfather Bat assured them, "We are not alone in the world, and we are far from defenseless. Now that we know the Buttinskys are a persistent threat, Gray

Squirrel can put the word out to our countless friends on the NNN."

Gray Squirrel's tiny jaw dropped. She really was living on the edge of history.

"What's the NNN?" Grampa Halfmoon asked.

"May I please exit my travel pouch?" she asked. At Grampa's soft grunt of approval, Gray Squirrel hopped onto Mel's lap and recited the information from memory. "The Nuts News Network is a brilliantly efficient squirrel-to-squirrel information relay system that stretches across the continent and is monitored by thousands of other species, even the most reclusive. Priority topics include human encroachment, climate change, and competitive sports. The squirrels rightly take pride in doing a bang-up job of it. Our eyes and ears are everywhere."

Although Grampa Halfmoon still had mixed feelings about it, he agreed to allow Mel and Ray to continue on the journey. He took 51 out of Tahlequah to 59 South through the Ozark National Forest. Mel spotted a Heritage Trail sign recognizing the Trail of Tears alongside the highway in Cedarville, Arkansas. Despite constantly scanning the surrounding landscape, that day none of them caught sight of the white van. They got on 40 East and after about an hour on the interstate, Ray asked, "How could the Buttinskys have found us in Cherokee Nation?"

Mel thought about it. The Buttinskys had already been

in the parking lot outside Iowa City before she, Ray, and Grampa Halfmoon had come out of the gas station convenience store. "They could've stuck a tracking device to the truck when we were in Iowa."

Ray pointed to a rest-stop sign along the highway. "Grampa, pull over there!"

Grampa Halfmoon was already signaling to exit.

The rest stop was well maintained, with a long, freshly marked parking lot and towering trees. A gray sedan, a red tractor trailer, and a blue eighteen-wheeler had been parked nearby, and a couple of senior citizens were entering the one-story building that was equipped with restrooms, tourism information, and vending machines.

As Grampa retrieved his flashlight from the glove compartment, Ray and Mel did their best to explain GPS tracking. "In space, in space!" Gray Squirrel kept repeating as she scurried underneath the truck, searching for anything out of the ordinary. "Satellites in space! In the sky, in the stars. In space! What's a satellite?"

Grampa Halfmoon shined the flashlight under the truck. "Look for a small black box. Tiny, even. It might have a light or an antenna on it."

Gray Squirrel peeked up at him from underneath the driver's-side wheelhouse. "What's an antenna?" Mel was running her fingertips along the right wheel fender, and Ray was skimming his along the grilles.

Grampa Halfmoon called to Gray Squirrel, "Why don't

you go ahead and notify the NNN of our Buttinsky problem?"

"Yes, sir! Absolutely, sir! I'm on it!" Gray Squirrel
replied, dashing across the grass. To herself, she added,
"Ha! They think they can track us. We'll track *them*!"

Our heroes checked the radiator and radiator supports,
the air-conditioning condenser, mirrors, headlights, tail-
gates, taillights, bumpers, bumper brackets, door panels,
and the rest of the fenders. Grampa Halfmoon had the
hood up and was inspecting the engine.

What's that, cousins? Y'all want to tell them to check
inside Bat's shoebox? You're wondering why that doesn't
occur to them? Well, think about it: so far as they know,
if the Buttinskys hid a tracker on Grampa's pickup, it
must've been in Iowa. How else could Midas, if it was
him, have located the vehicle in the Berghoffs' driveway?
After all, when Grampa went into the convenience store
in Iowa City, he'd left only the driver's-side window open
a crack for Gray Squirrel. There was no possible way that
Midas could've reached through that little opening to
affix anything.

Mel said, "As long as we're here, I'm taking a restroom
break."

"Me too." Ray asked his grandfather, "You coming?"

"Hang on, I have an idea." Grampa Halfmoon clicked
off the flashlight and, while Ray and Mel were inside, he
fetched the car jack from the back of the truck to take a

long, careful look underneath the pickup.

"Any luck?" Bat asked a few moments later.

Grampa Halfmoon shook his head. "If there was a trackin' device, maybe it fell off. We've come a long way since Iowa City, and there are plenty of potholes in that long driveway to Wilhelmina and Leonard's house."

⚝ 15 ⚝

BUTTING IN AGAIN

Gray Squirrel returned to the rest stop about half an hour later. "Mission accomplished!"

"Good job," Grampa Halfmoon said. What a blessing it was that she'd come along!

Sitting on the hood of the truck, Mel asked, "Do any other land species have a relay system?"

Ray tossed his lemon-lime soda can into a recycling bin. "Besides squirrels and humans?"

"Just one," Great-Grandfather Bat put in. "But they keep to themselves."

That afternoon, riding in Grampa Halfmoon's truck, Ray didn't draw, and Mel didn't read. The only thing they could figure was that the Buttinskys had been chasing them by old-fashioned sight, and our heroes simply hadn't noticed. They'd believed that they'd escaped Midas and Truly in Iowa City, so it's not like our heroes had been watching out for the white van previously.

For hours, Mel and Ray and the animals stared out the truck windows at other vehicles on the highway. White vans were common, though, so there were a couple of false alarms—one van belonging to a florist shop and another van belonging to an exterminator service. Ray also noticed a few adopt-a-highway signs and the remains of an armadillo who'd met a tragic fate.

High above, clouds gathered, and the sky began to drizzle. Mel's mind wandered to what Great-Grandfather Bat had said about a tear in her heart, how spending time on her ancestral land could help mend it. It had sounded so strange to hear him put it that way. Mel had never thought of *herself* as having been ripped away—that tragedy had happened generations ago to other people. But what if it had never happened? When she imagined centuries of Muscogee people, immersed in their thriving culture, thousands of them fluent in their tribal language, she couldn't help feeling the ache of loss.

Mel prayed quietly to the Creator for healing. She prayed quietly that Bat had been right.

Nearing Memphis, our heroes found themselves in a traffic snarl. Then, when that cleared, Grampa Halfmoon honked sharply twice at a semi that had wandered into the center lane beside them. He wasn't one to complain, but the driving was beginning to wear on him. His lower back felt sore. This last stretch would be even longer if they got caught in traffic in Atlanta, Georgia. And Grampa wasn't altogether sure how to find the traditional playing field from there. Better that they get a good night's sleep and hit the road fresh in the morning.

Grampa navigated through crop fields and dense trees, past ponds and over creeks. "Any luck finding us a place to bed down?"

"Yep," Ray replied, using his phone to research their lodging options. "But we won't be camping. We'll be *glamping* on farmland outside the city."

"Glamping?" Grampa Halfmoon pulled into a gas station to scrub the bug guts off the windshield and fuel up for the next day. Grampa had heard of glamping, or glamorous camping. It sounded to him like a way for wealthy folks to playact camping. Not that he was a snob about not being a snob. Grampa had an adaptable personality and he enjoyed fancy digs as much as the next person. The lodging was more expensive than the state park in Missouri, but the cost was about what he'd been expecting to pay for a roadside hotel chain. Besides, he had a feeling that Mel had roughed it enough for one trip. "All righty," he said. "It's a plan."

A hefty, wide-shouldered bridge, outlined in rivets, welcomed the truck over the Mississippi River to the state of Tennessee. From there, it was a short jog from the other side of Memphis into the state of Mississippi, where they planned to bed down for the night.

Before exiting the highway for the day, Grampa Halfmoon had decided to splurge on a family-size order of fast-food fried chicken with green beans, fried okra, and corn bread. Our heroes took it with them to a farm, where they were greeted by a middle-aged couple. She was a white woman with teased gray hair who wore a Dolly Parton T-shirt decorated with rhinestones, and he was a Korean-American man with an army tattoo on his forearm who wore a faded Memphis Bigfoot Festival T-shirt.

"Welcome! I'm Tammy, and that's my darling Dale," she said, gesturing to her husband. "It's always been our dream to host travelers out here. You're our very first customers."

Which explained why it was so affordable, Grampa Halfmoon realized. Like Little Mac back in Missouri, they were trying to attract business and build word of mouth. He liked supporting small local businesses. "Nice to meet you," he replied, after introducing Ray and Mel as his grandkids. Meanwhile, Gray Squirrel was outside surveying the property from the treetops.

"We're from Chicago," Ray added. "Home of the Chicago Cubs."

"A baseball fan!" Dale reached for Grampa Halfmoon's roller bag. "Here, I'll take that. It's a short hike to the tent."

By *a short hike*, he meant about twenty minutes across what used to be a cow pasture. Ray and Mel carried their backpacks. Gray Squirrel followed from a casual distance, and Grampa Halfmoon brought Bat in his shoebox, so Dale was none the wiser. Along the way, the glamp-ground owner explained that he and Tammy planned to add bike rentals and either paintball or laser tag to lure in guests. Ray voted for paintball, Mel voted for laser tag, and Grampa pointed out the expense of having to keep restocking paint.

"Fancy!" Grampa Halfmoon exclaimed when they arrived at their destination.

The large, heavy tent was situated on a newly constructed, elevated wooden deck a short distance from the tree line and a pond. "Fully stocked," Dale promised, unzipping the accommodations. "It's supposed to rain off and on until sunrise. Nothing serious. Tammy signed us up for satellite internet, if you need it. It's slow, but it's better than nothing. Tomorrow morning, I'll introduce you to our permanent residents—we've got chickens, goats, ducks, and a miniature donkey named Jolene." He smiled at that. "If you circle around the rear of the tent, you'll find an outdoor shower and a modern outhouse— built 'em myself—with a compost toilet. Y'all have a good night."

With that, he was off. Grampa stepped inside the tent and rubbed his hands together. "This sure is somethin'!" The tent had been furnished in white wicker with a full-size bed, a sofa bed, a nightstand with a Bible on it, a breakfast table, and a coffee table. It was decorated in pastel fabrics with a large floral rug and fresh peonies.

There was a freestanding privacy screen in the far right-hand corner and a cushy lounge chair big enough for

Mel to sleep on. She set her backpack next to it.

Gray Squirrel popped her upside-down furry face through the tent flaps. "All clear!"

"Why don't you and Bat stay with us in here tonight?" Grampa Halfmoon said, opening the shoebox. "Just don't chew on the furniture." At that, Great-Grandfather Bat looked vaguely affronted, and Gray Squirrel looked vaguely disappointed, but there was something sweet about them all spending their last night before the big game together.

Gray Squirrel darted around the tent, investigating, before sprinting back to the entrance. "Does anyone smell motor oil? I smell motor oil."

Grampa Halfmoon set Bat's box on the white wicker coffee table. But Bat was already crawling around the tent supports, seeking a higher, safer place to tuck himself in. Then it occurred to him how much love and effort Ray had put into decorating the box and how Grampa Halfmoon had provided him with a bounty of regularly changed, luxurious bedding. Once the human cubs began readying themselves for sleep, Bat planned to snuggle into it one last time.

Grampa grabbed a handful of raw pecans and a couple of apples from the care package Aunt Wilhelmina had sent with them. He was starting to second-guess himself. Grampa was thinking he should've told Ray to reserve a room at a hotel where there would be security cameras and a front-desk clerk who could be on the lookout for people fitting the description of the Buttinskys. But no, he was just being a worrywart, he told himself. Our heroes had kept close watch for that day's leg of the trip. No way could the white van have been chasing them by sight. He and Bat had scoured every centimeter of the pickup. There was no tracking device attached to the truck. The kids were safe. Bat and Gray Squirrel were safe.

At that very moment, Truly and Midas drove past Tammy and Dale's place for the third time. "What do you mean, the tracking signal doesn't point to the house or the pickup truck?" she scolded. "Where else could they be?"

Midas was using two fingers to zero in on the location dot on his screen. "Out there in the woods somewhere," he said. "Which is perfect. You didn't want to try approaching them again this morning back in Oklahoma—"

"Those enormous hogs could've been waiting for us!" Truly exclaimed. "Did you see the tusks on those monsters?" They'd been cycling on the conversation for hours. She added, "Daylight's wasting. How far away is the signal's origin point?"

Grampa Halfmoon returned to the glamping tent after setting out pecans and a couple of apples on a stump near the tree line. Mel realized she'd been so distracted by the threat of the Buttinskys and by reflecting on her ancestral land that receiving her cousin's text message had slipped her mind. She piped up from the sofa. "Last night, Rain sent me a link to a video," she said, tapping her screen to watch. It took forever and ever and ever to load. Blinking at the cover image, Mel exclaimed, "It's *us*!"

"What do you mean *us*?" Ray asked, sitting next to her to watch.

Mel pointed at the viewer count. "Check out those numbers—it's viral!" She tapped play and it buffered, so she tapped pause to wait while everyone else gathered closer to see for themselves. They waited a while longer in silence. Finally, *finally*, Mel tapped play again.

Gray Squirrel was bouncing on top of the cushion behind them. She had seen moving pictures before, of course. But this one was hilarious. It opened with a view of a crowded room of humans talking and eating. Then came the voice. "Chewie boy!" The bounding black dog from Kansas had accidentally caused a chaotic chain of events that ultimately led to red goo splattering all over Grampa Halfmoon and a human woman.

Depending on Great-Grandfather Bat's mood, he felt that it was either quaint or distressing that humans obsessed over their handheld tools when they could've been soaking up the wonders of the natural world. But he adored *these* humans and the antics of the dog in Kansas had entertained him, too, so in this case, he found their behavior charming.

"May I see that?" Grampa Halfmoon asked. It was a short video clip, he noticed. He and Georgia had laughed about that moment all night. The date had been a huge success. In fact, Grampa had received a text from her that morning, confirming that she'd done him the favor of sending a copy of the picture book *Fry Bread: A Native American Family Story* to Little Mac's kids in gratitude for going the extra mile, so to speak, in giving them a ride to the Missouri state park and getting the pickup repaired so fast. Grampa realized that whoever had happened to capture his date night must've had the camera pointed at him and Georgia already, a fact that he'd be sure to ask her about later.

Then he noticed that the video had been tagged to Tricia's Barbecue House. That's when the pieces began falling into place. Hannesburg was small, and the Berghoff house was located in the historic district, close to the old downtown. Grampa Halfmoon didn't regret putting the #LandBack bumper sticker on his truck, but that did make it easier for someone to confirm it was his. "This video could be how the Buttinskys located us in Kansas."

"What about from Cousin Rain's house to Aunt Wilhelmina and Uncle Leonard's?" Ray asked. "There were miles at a stretch when the highway was basically empty. We made a few pit stops. It seems like one of us would've noticed their white van." Especially since it was an off-road van, not a standard one. That made it taller and meant the body of the vehicle looked jacked up above the wheels. Ray added, "At the rest stop, we went over every inch of the pickup."

"Could they have put something *inside* the truck?" Bat

asked. "Ray, you did leave a window down for me and Gray Squirrel to slip into the trees after the picnic outside Mel's kin's roost. That night, Midas—if that was him—was lurking near the truck."

"We would've noticed if he'd snuck a tracker into the back," Mel said. "We've spent hours—days—in the back seat. I've basically got it memorized."

"Me too," Ray put in. "Me too!" Gray Squirrel said.

Suddenly, Bat flew to his box and moved the latest thick terry-cloth dish towel. He clawed at the black liner made from a trash bag, revealing a small square stuck in place with double-sided adhesive. Because the liner had been attached at the corners, not all the way around, there were openings big enough to insert the tracker. "I never noticed it," Bat said. "I never felt it."

"We've kept it well padded," Mel pointed out. "Besides, you haven't spent as much time in there since your wing healed."

Grampa Halfmoon plucked the plastic rectangle from the cardboard. "I hate to say it, but if this gadget is what we think it is, the Buttinskys already know we're here."

Ping, sounded Grampa's phone. "It's a message from Leonard. A neighbor found a video camera and microphone along the side of the road leading to their house."

At that moment, our heroes heard vehicle doors slam shut. Ray and Mel rushed to the open tent flaps. A familiar all-terrain white van was parked on the incline overlooking the pond. By the light of the setting sun, the Buttinskys were charging the glamping site.

"It's them!" Mel exclaimed. "They're here."

"The Buttinskys are here?" Gray Squirrel asked.

"They're coming this way!" Ray added.

Grampa Halfmoon had had enough. He was a humble man, a tool of the Creator. Every day, in ways small and large, he showed the grandkids how to live a good life.

Grampa said a quick, quiet prayer for strength of character, for patience, and for protection. He resolved to use his words and let his faith guide him through the confrontation to come. No way around it—the Buttinskys were bullies. They were stalkers. All they cared about was attracting visitors to their web show to make money. Too many fine folks had fallen victim to their harassment, and poor Bat had suffered a frightening captivity at their hands. Grampa glanced over his shoulder at Bat, Gray Squirrel, and the grandchildren. "Y'all stay here. I'll handle this."

As Grampa exited the tent, Truly raised a newly purchased replacement camera and, walking backward, Midas turned his back on the glamping tent to speak to the lens. "Buckle up for the Buttinsky Bulletin! This is Midas Buttinsky, coming to you with the Buttinsky Bulletin—where I *butt in* for a good cause. Today we're on the far side of Memphis, following up on the talking bat—"

"Cut!" Truly lowered the camera. "Midas, we've

discussed this. We've been over and over it. We're going with the exotic-animal-trade angle, not that talking-bat nonsense."

"Truly, I swear to you—"

"I don't rightly care what your angle is," Grampa Halfmoon called. "Either you two pack up and vamoose or you're goin' to be in a mess of trouble." He hadn't meant to sound so gruff, but when emotions are running high, the best of intentions can go awry.

"How do you figure that, animal abuser?" Truly yelled, raising the camera again. Midas might get on her very last nerve, but they had a job to do.

Mel stepped out of the tent and stood to one side of Grampa with Gray Squirrel on her right shoulder. Ray stepped out of the tent and stood to the other side of Grampa with Bat on his left shoulder. They were defying Grampa Halfmoon's orders, but they had come this far together and, until Bat was delivered to the traditional playing fields, together they would remain.

"They have a squirrel, too," Truly told her brother. "If anybody cares about squirrels."

"Two!" Midas exclaimed, coming around the pond. "They have *two* wild animals. Their operation is even bigger than we feared." Still addressing the camera lens, he added, "We are hereby confiscating the bat and squirrel. We demand that you surrender them to us immediately."

"Um," Mel whispered, catching sight of a large, hulking

silhouette along the tree line. She tilted her head in that direction. Voice low, she added, *"Over there!"* Gray Squirrel and Great-Grandfather Bat caught the familiar scent, and it wasn't the Buttinskys. Grampa Halfmoon glanced at the figure in the forest and, with a hint of a grin, slightly raised his chin. "You're outnumbered," he said.

"And outclassed," Bat added.

Still filming, Truly yammered, "It, it *does* talk. The bat. It's *talking*. That's, that's amazing! Bubba, I'm sorry I doubted you. So help me, I never imagined such a thing." She hadn't called her brother Bubba since they'd been children. Moving to an angle where the lens would better show both our heroes and her brother, Truly checked to make sure her camera was still recording. It was.

Midas was persistent, but he wasn't much of a planner. Normally, for web episodes, he preferred public locations and interventions sure to attract a crowd. He drew on their energy, created a spectacle. He'd puff himself up and bluster his way through one mess after another, all of his own making. Usually, by this point, he was being chased away and tossing off one-liners about how his latest victims would rue the day. But this was secluded, private property. Lacking any better ideas, he kept talking. "You two kids put together don't equal an adult."

"Maybe, maybe not," Ray said. "But the two of you put together are no match for, uh—" He pointed behind Midas and Truly across the pond at the large, dark figure taking long, purposeful strides toward the rear of the white van.

Midas laughed. "What? Someone's behind me. You think I'd fall for that old trick?"

Long Man? Mel thought, her knees trembling. *Tall Man? Este Capko?*

He opened his jaws, releasing another echoing holler—a *hoop, hoop, hoop*ing sound. At seven, nine feet—maybe more; it was hard to tell at that angle and distance—the hairy new arrival was all muscle, indignation, and, against all odds, wearing what used to be Grampa Halfmoon's lucky fishing hat. He began running with huge strides, faster and more nimble than y'all would expect from anyone so big and bulky. He shoved the Buttinskys' van, which careened down the incline and fell—*ka-splash!*—into the pond. The creature opened his square jaws, releasing another echoing holler. A big noise exploding from big lungs. From the distance, an identical call responded.

"It—it's not an ape," Truly said as gurgling bubbles rose to the water's surface and the van began to sink. "That, that noise, though. Primate?"

"Not a bear," Midas replied. "It's walking on two legs. Bears can do that, but—"

"Definitely not a bear," his sister confirmed. "No ape I've ever seen." For a moment, the siblings' eyes met, and they reflected at each other with dollar signs. Truly pointed her camera lens at the furry figure, which ran off, taking refuge in the trees that it came from.

The Buttinsky siblings gave chase—their van forgotten, our heroes forgotten, no longer caring a lick about a talking-bat web episode or illegal-animal-trading web episode. As far as Midas and Truly were concerned, from that moment on, their life's mission would be to apprehend and cash in on a living legend.

Gray Squirrel cocked her head. "What if they trap—"

"Don't worry," Bat said. "So many humans have tried and failed. . . ."

Mel gently scratched under Gray Squirrel's chin. "Those losers don't stand a chance."

"That hat?" Ray said in a quiet voice. "Your lucky hat."

Grampa Halfmoon slowly shook his head. "Mysteries abound."

⚹ 16 ⚹

GAME DAY

On Thursday morning, Tammy and Dale served up spinach, mushroom, and goat-cheese omelets with crispy home fries. They took news of the white van in their pond in stride. "That's why we started this business," Dale said. "Every day brings surprises. Stories to tell our future grandkids."

Before leaving, Grampa Halfmoon used his phone to leave glowing reviews for Little Mac's Auto Body Shop and for Tammy & Dale's Glamping Tents. Grampa also asked Tammy for a stamp and envelope. He slipped the Buttinskys' tracking device inside it, addressed it to a local hazardous waste disposal facility, and dropped it in the mailbox on the way out.

Grampa Halfmoon took I-22 through Holly Springs National Forest into Alabama through the big city of Birmingham, to I-20 East through Talladega National

Forest and into Georgia.

The sun was shining, the sky was clear, and every time Grampa Halfmoon got out of the pickup, his glasses fogged in the humidity. Our heroes went past so many churches on the trip. They didn't even try to keep count. But Grampa did turn up Dolly Parton's "Jesus & Gravity" on the radio. As they progressed, our heroes spotted Confederate flags harkening to the US Civil War of the 1860s, some thirty years after the Trail of Tears. They recalled their southeastern tribes' shameful history of slavery as well as their kinship and cultural ties to the enslaved Black people and their Freedmen descendants. This was the first time Mel and Ray had been south of Oklahoma.

Even Gray Squirrel was bored by all the trees. She asked, "Are we there yet?"

Grampa Halfmoon chuckled. "Almost, my friend. We've still got Atlanta ahead."

Mel's phone vibrated—it was a text from her dad.

Your mom has been sending me updates about your spring-break adventure. She says you're going home to your Muscogee lands. I'm grateful to your ancestors for giving the world your mother, and I'm grateful to her for giving me you. I love you, Melanie Melody.

Mel felt somehow lighter and more solid at the same time. Her dad should've checked in more often. His new job and new family were no excuse. Life was change. But he was still her father, and she was still his daughter, and he wasn't the only one whose life was different. Mel had embraced new adventures, too. She wrote back, *I love you, too*.

Raising her gaze from the screen, Mel asked her companions, "Do you figure the Buttinskys will ever give up on chasing you-know-who and decide to bother us again?"

Ray said, "Truly was filming when Bat said a few words."

Great-Grandfather Bat was snuggled against Ray's jawline. "Now that I'm fully healed, they'll never find—let alone *catch*—me again."

Up in the driver's seat, Grampa Halfmoon added, "Even if they do post that video, viewers will probably write it off to a trick of technology."

Gray Squirrel swallowed a chewed-up hazelnut from the pet-store bag. "Animals talk all the time. All the time! Well, not all the time. Sometimes we sleep or we're extra quiet—"

"What're you getting at?" Bat nudged.

She focused. "All I'm saying is, the fact that we're not speaking human language doesn't mean we're not . . ." Gray Squirrel searched her memory for the word. "Communicating."

"Valid point," Mel said.

"I apologize," Grampa Halfmoon replied. "I should've said, 'Folks would probably figure the Buttinskys used a tech trick to make it look like Bat was speaking the

English human language.' From now on, I'll take extra care to show respect for how animals communicate."

"Especially squirrels and bats," Gray Squirrel pointed out.

"Especially squirrels and bats," Grampa Halfmoon promised good-naturedly.

"Wado, Gray Squirrel," Ray put in. She had matured over the course of the journey. Maybe they all had. Soon they would arrive at the traditional playing field, and after the game, it would be time to say farewell to her and Great-Grandfather Bat. Ray missed them already.

❧ 17 ❧

HOME FIELD

That afternoon, Mel's mom texted a photo of herself in the bleachers at the Cubs' season opener, with Dalton, Luis, and Luis's mom. Ray still longed for more of a connection with the father he knew only through stories, but after talking to Uncle Leonard, he felt his dad's presence more than he ever had before. Maybe Ray wasn't at Wrigley Field today, but he'd played an important role in delivering Great-Grandfather Bat to an even more important ball game. "I'm glad they're having fun," Ray said, returning the phone.

As Grampa Halfmoon had feared, they caught sight of the Atlanta skyline around rush hour. It took a while to pass through the city—what with the slow-and-go traffic on 75 South—and Mel was grateful that Grampa Halfmoon was such a skilled defensive driver.

"Whoa!" Gray Squirrel and Ray exclaimed as a jet flew low across the highway.

"Please tell me the airport is nearby," Mel said.

"The airport is nearby," Great-Grandfather Bat replied. It had been a challenge to his senses, traveling this way, but now—traffic permitting—they'd arrive at their destination soon.

Once they'd passed through the city of McDonough, Bat called, "Charlie, could you please exit the highway and find a place to sit a spell while I fly up for a better idea of where we are?"

Our heroes ended up outside Macon at another gas station with a convenience store—the same sort of place as the one outside Iowa City. Grampa Halfmoon parked the pickup at the far end of the asphalt lot, and without warning, Bat flew out of Ray's window.

"Bat is coming back, isn't he?" Mel asked.

"He's coming back!" Gray Squirrel assured her. "I'm going with him to the big game. I may not be an athlete, but I can lead the cheering section."

Great-Grandfather Bat returned within the hour, reporting that for Gray Squirrel to make the trek to the traditional playing field, they would need to continue to the other side of nearby Macon to a gorgeous, wooded landscape, which Grampa Halfmoon was quick to identify as in the general area of Ocmulgee Mounds National Historical Park.

"Right up there," Bat said, fluttering to the top of the dashboard and using a wing to point Grampa Halfmoon in the direction of the turnoff. Then Bat hopped onto the back of the empty front passenger seat headrest to address Gray Squirrel. "How do you feel about riding Deer?"

Gray Squirrel had met deer before in Albany Park and in Cherokee Nation. Would it be rude to suggest a camel instead? "What other animals are approaching the traditional playing field?"

"Fast and big enough to carry you?" he replied. "Fox, Bear, Bobcat—"

"Deer sounds good," Gray Squirrel replied, still skittish around predators.

Grampa Halfmoon pulled off the highway onto a backwoods road. Sure enough, there was White-Tailed Deer, grazing with deliberate casualness. Grampa left a respectful distance between him and the pickup truck. Everyone got out, and Grampa Halfmoon said the tough words so Bat wouldn't have to. "Kids, we're not going to Bat's ball game. It's an occasion strictly for the Animals and the Birds. It's up to them to tell humans what, if anything, they decide is okay to share about the rematch and when it'll be okay to share it. We have our own ball games, traditional and otherwise. We need to show our respect by stepping away now."

From Ray's shoulder, Bat said, "Charlie, from one grandfather to another, I must say, you are exceptional. It's been an honor. Donadagohvi."

Grampa Halfmoon replied, "Take care, my friend, till we meet again."

With that, Great-Grandfather Bat addressed Mel and Ray. "You two listen to your Elders, take care of the land, of the water, of the sky, and give my best to Bandit and Dragon." Bat wasn't the type to hold grudges, even against house cats. "Mvto. Wado."

"I'll see you again," Mel replied, eyes misty.

"Yeah," Ray said. "Good luck in the big game! We're rooting for you."

Then it was time for farewells to Gray Squirrel, except her head was buried in Mel's neck. No one was in a hurry. A moment or two passed, and then she said, "I want to go home."

"To Chicago?" Mel asked, not surprised. Home could have a powerful pull on the heart.

Gray Squirrel added, "But I want to go to the ball game, too. Bat needs me!"

Grampa Halfmoon said, "Little one, you don't have to choose." Raising his voice so White-Tailed Deer could hear, he said, "We've come a long, long way, and we're not in a big hurry to leave the area. Could you meet us here tomorrow between midday and evening?"

Gray Squirrel's tail twitched with joy. "You won't forget me?"

"Never," Mel and Ray promised at the same time.

Through the windshield of the pickup, the Halfmoons

and Mel watched Great-Grandfather Bat take flight and Gray Squirrel ride off on the back of White-Tailed Deer. "Woo-hoo!" Gray Squirrel chattered. "Team Animals forever!"

"Don't we have to leave right away?" Ray was confused. "It took us nearly a week to get here, and we're supposed to be back in school on Monday."

Grampa started the ignition. "We spent nearly a week getting here because we took the scenic route, spent time with loved ones, and ran into few hiccups along the way. My plan is to take off again tomorrow afternoon after we pick up Gray Squirrel. On our return trip, I'll point the pickup northwest and keep on truckin' up through Tennessee, Kentucky, and Indiana, all the way to Chicago. It's slightly more than thirteen hours over three days." He patted the steering wheel. "This old girl is runnin' smooth as silk. With no bat-napping, no family time—"

"No romance," Mel teased. "No splattering barbecue sauce."

"No mysterious visitors from the forest?" Ray asked.

Grampa Halfmoon chuckled, driving back to the main road. "Well, I can't promise all that. But we won't have to push too hard, and you'll be in Mrs. Flores's class come Monday."

The next day, the Halfmoons accompanied Mel to the Ocmulgee Mounds on land that had been home to her ancestors. They stood side by side, near the visitor center, on a paved path that led down, down, down a hill to a small wooden bridge, and up, up, up a hill to living history, to grassy green earthen mounds on land where Native peoples had lived for thousands of years. Then settlers brought suffering and enslavement, the loss of land and lives. Our heroes erred on the side of quiet to give the experience room to breathe.

Y'all will believe me when I say it was a lot to take in. Yes, the Muscogee survivors of removal, of the Trail of Tears, had rebuilt their tribal Nation on what was once called Indian Territory and was now surrounded by the borders of Oklahoma. Yes, Mel also thought of her father's Odawa community in Michigan as home, too, especially when she was at her grandparents' house, and she still thought of Kalamazoo as home, as well. Lately, she had come to feel at home in the Halfmoon bungalow, too.

And yet, this place, this moment, harkened to echoes of her dreams and a shimmer beyond her horizon. Sure, our heroes had been on rightful Muscogee land since yesterday, had visited a gas station on that land, had ridden in Grampa Halfmoon's truck across that land, had enjoyed fried green tomatoes at a retro diner built on that land, and had spent last night at Millie's Micro Motel on that land. But in this place, in this ancient place, the rhythm of the rolling green land beat like a drum in her heart.

Mel whispered, "I feel like I should've been here before, should've always lived here or at least been born here. I should *know* it. I should be able to remember this land." Were her ancestors watching, listening? Were those their voices singing with Wind?

She was French, Odawa, and Muscogee by heritage—American and Muscogee by citizenship. Did her ancestors recognize her? Here, there, and always? Of course they did.

To either side of Mel, Ray and Grampa Halfmoon offered their hands, and she gripped them, gasping at the rising emotion, the way tears dotted her cheeks. Was she grieving for what had been stolen? Mel repeated, "I should be able to remember this land."

Ray thought back to the bear hug that he'd received from Uncle Leonard in Cherokee Nation. He thought about what Uncle Leonard had said about Ray and the parents he'd lost so long ago. "That's okay," Ray told Mel. "The land remembers you."

GLOSSARY

CHEROKEE–ENGLISH
donadagohvi/ᏦᎤᎦᏕᏬᎢ (do-nuh-daw-gō-huh-ee):
until we meet again
osiyo/ᎣᏏᏲ (O-see-YO): hello
wado/ᎬᎥ (wah-dō): thank you

MVSKOKE–ENGLISH
Este Capko (est-e chep-ko): Tall Man/Person (also
called Bigfoot)
hesci (hens-jay): hello
mvto (muh-dō): thank you
okmulgee (oak-MULL-ghee): bubbling waters

OJIBWE–ENGLISH
Anishinaabemowin (an-ish-naw-BAY-moō-win): the
language of the Ojibwe people

A NOTE FROM THE AUTHOR

All of Creation is connected through circles. Circles of life, of community, of generations, and of the earth rotating through space and time. If overlapping circles have the power to harm, like those of Indigenous peoples and of colonizers, then that power should be repurposed to heal.

Story is a key to that healing. The circle of story is big and strong enough to hold all of who we are, who we have been, and who we should be. The circle of story is good medicine.

In this novel, Grampa Halfmoon circles back to his sweetheart, Ray to the love of his parents, and Mel to her ancestral homeland. Bat circles back to his sports days, and Gray Squirrel circles to the hero within. None of them makes their journey alone. As they travel together, Mel and Ray are guided by Grampa Halfmoon. Gray Squirrel is guided by Great-Grandfather Bat. If you need it, I hope this book guides you in some way.

Like we're all connected to one another, the characters and places in my stories are connected, too. For example, readers of my books may be familiar with the Story of Bat from its mention in the picture book *Jingle Dancer* and with Ray and Grampa Halfmoon from my chapter book, *Indian Shoes*. You can find out how Ray and Mel first met and became friends in my short story "Between the Lines," which appears in the anthology *Ancestor Approved: Intertribal Stories for Kids*. If you want to read a story about Mel's cousin Rain in Kansas, you might also check out *Rain Is Not My Indian Name*.

Sometimes people ask me why certain fictional families reappear in my books.

My motto is: Every kid can be a hero that everybody cheers. *Every kid* includes Indigenous kids, both real ones and make-believe ones like the characters in my stories.

But there aren't enough Native people in books or on television or in the movies—not enough real-life ones and not enough make-believe ones—not yet. Meanwhile, you have opportunities to enjoy lots of stories about non-Native real-life heroes, like Sammy Sosa and Dolly Parton, through nonfiction, and make-believe heroes, like R2-D2 and Wonder Woman, through fiction. You feel like you know them, and in a way, you do. There's a *relationship* there, one built over time and through repeated connections. Whether you are Native or not, my hope is that by connecting again and again with my characters, you'll build a relationship with them, and, from there, you'll feel a positive connection to Native people both in real life and on the page.

Speaking of make-believe, as you already know, the depictions of the animals in this book are heavily fictionalized. These characters pay tribute to a long tradition of Muscogee storytelling—and Native storytelling more broadly—about games played by Birds and Animals. You should not expect any wild animals you encounter to behave the way they're shown here. Do not handle or otherwise interact with them like Mel, Ray, and Grampa Halfmoon do. Wild animals should be respected and protected from a distance.

This novel itself isn't an age-old traditional story or a retelling of an age-old traditional story, though it does have roots in cultural tradition. It's fiction but not fantasy. Navajo children's author Brian Young refers to this type of story as modern folklore.

Today, Muscogee people gather around fires and kitchen tables sharing all kinds of tales, including ones about a creature you may know as Bigfoot or Sasquatch—a creature that has shared the land for countless generations and may have much to teach us if we're ready to listen. No, there's no hard proof of their existence, but maybe the truth is somehow bigger than that. Maybe it's about the way Este Capko embodies the natural places most humans don't—and maybe shouldn't—visit. Or at least those we should travel with the utmost care.

The Muscogee Trail of Tears of the 1830s is real Muscogee history and real United States history. Shorter relocation to the west in the years leading up to it were a reality, too. For countless generations the Muscogee lived within the borders of what's now Alabama and Georgia, and the Nation included enslaved people of African descent. Their perilous removal to Indian Territory, now Oklahoma, happened over hundreds of miles by land and water. Families took only what they could carry and lacked warm clothing to protect them against the winter cold. Thousands of all ages suffered and died on the journey.

That said, this novel isn't a retracing of any of the removal routes. Rather, it's a fictional story that brings our heroes from Chicago to the Ocmulgee Mounds.

They're not the only ones who took that road trip. Authors can't always travel to the places where our stories are set, but doing so can offer us insights and information— lived experiences and details—that make our books even better. With my husband, I took a flight from Austin, Texas, to Chicago. We rented a car, and over the course of six days—from Saturday to Thursday, sticking to the schedule in the book—we drove to Macon, Georgia. That weekend we visited the Ocmulgee Mounds. My initial thought was that that experience would be a healing one for Mel. I didn't realize how much the same would be true for me.

To say the Ocmulgee Mounds of the Mississippian Mound Culture predate the removal era is an understatement. But it's important to know that it's a place of *living* Indigenous history, living Indigenous culture. For example, at the annual Ocmulgee Indigenous Celebration, many of today's Muscogee come home to engage in music and dance, educational programs, food, crafts, storytelling, and much more. The site has been designated Ocmulgee Mounds National Historical Park since 2019 and previously was established by US President Franklin Roosevelt as Ocmulgee National Monument. I had a wonderful experience at the Ocmulgee Visitor Center and was pleased to find a prominent display of large photographs of modern-day Muscogee people that ensure everyone knows we're still here.

In this story, the focus is more on land than the mounds specifically, although they're of course inseparable. However, the mounds are sacred and fascinating. If you're interested in learning more about them, you may want to visit the websites both of Ocmulgee Mounds National Historical Park and of the Smithsonian National Museum of the American Indian.

The modern Muscogee Nation is located within the borders of Oklahoma. At the time of this book's original publication—with about one hundred thousand citizens—it is one of the ten largest sovereign Indigenous Nations on the continent. The descendants of the enslaved survivors of the Trail of Tears are the Muscogee Freedmen. Relatives of the Muscogee known as the Poarch Band of Creek Indians are located today within Alabama, having escaped removal due to either their relationships to the US government or their employment as scouts and traders, resulting in land grants.

In this story, the family homes, Ray and Mel's school, and the small businesses are made up. So is the historic town of Hannesburg, Kansas. Mel and Ray are young students of their respective Native Nations' histories. Grampa Halfmoon is a history buff. But none of them are experts. That said, Grampa is a supporter of the #LandBack movement, which advances the idea of rejecting colonialist systems so that, among other changes, Native Nations will be restored as the caretakers of their traditional territories. However, it would be unrealistic for the characters to pinpoint every tribal land relationship along their route, and the sharing of all that information would be a book unto itself. To learn more, you could read related works by citizens/members of the respective Nations and visit the tribes' official websites, which may include cultural and historical resources.

I encourage you to read Indigenous books, too. In this story, Mel reads middle grade books by Swampy Cree author David A. Robertson. Mel also gives her cousins a few picture books by author Kim Rogers of Wichita and Affiliated Tribes, and Georgia helps out Grampa

Halfmoon by sending a picture book, *Fry Bread: A Native American Family Story*, by Seminole author Kevin Noble Maillard and Peruvian-born illustrator Juana Martinez-Neal, to Little Mac as a thank-you for fixing the pickup truck. If you're interested in reading historical fiction about removal, I recommend *Mary and the Trail of Tears* by Cherokee author Andrea L. Rogers, which is based on her tribe's history.

Mvto, thank you, for joining me in the circle of story. Best wishes on all your road trips, at all your ball games, and at all your homecomings. Many blessings.

ACKNOWLEDGMENTS

My gratitude to my editor, Rosemary Brosnan, whose professional excellence, sharp eye, and commitment to the emotional and intellectual needs of young readers is an ongoing source of guidance and inspiration; to my literary agent, Ginger Knowlton, who has been a steadfast companion and amazing advocate on a long and storied creative journey; and to my husband, Christopher, whose ongoing personal support as well as his driving prowess and photography-videography skills were a boon to my research and writing process.

Thank you to production editor Mikayla Lawrence, designer Andrea Vandergrift, cover artist Natasha Donovan, and Patty Rosati and her team at HarperCollins.

Thanks also to my author's assistant, Gayleen Rabakukk; James T. Farrell of Curtis Brown; Courtney Stevenson of Heartdrum / HarperCollins Children's Books; and those dear ones who spoke to me in depth about many of the topics—both weighty and hilarious—touched upon in the story.

A shout-out to the community of authors and illustrators of Austin, of the Vermont College of Fine Arts MFA program in Writing for Children and Young Adults, and of the We Need Diverse Books Native Children's-YA Writing Intensive, as well as to my fellow writers and artists creating Indigenous books for young readers more broadly. Plus, thanks to Ocmulgee Mounds Park Guide Andrea Martinson for her hospitality.

My journey in writing this story was likewise aided by animal heroes. Gnocchi came to me from an animal shelter in Austin. She is a deceptively adorable land shark disguised as a long-haired black Chihuahua. Orzo came to me from an animal shelter in San Marcos, Texas. He is a fluffy gold cuddle nugget disguised as a Pomeranian-Chihuahua mix. Together, they have taught me so much about patience and love, and they put in hours listening to me read scenes in progress, including a start-to-finish read-aloud of the entire manuscript.

Finally, I send my love, gratitude, and solidarity to the teachers, librarians, and booksellers who are connecting books like this one to the young readers who need them most.

ABOUT THE AUTHOR

CYNTHIA LEITICH SMITH is the bestselling, acclaimed author of books for all ages, including *Sisters of the Neversea*, *Rain Is Not My Indian Name*, *Indian Shoes*, *Jingle Dancer*, *Harvest House*, and *Hearts Unbroken*, which won the American Indian Library Association's Youth Literature Award; she is also the anthologist of *Ancestor Approved: Intertribal Stories for Kids*. She has been named the NSK Neustadt Laureate. Cynthia is the author-curator of Heartdrum, a Native-focused imprint at HarperCollins Children's Books, and has served as the Katherine Paterson Inaugural Endowed Chair on the faculty of the MFA program in Writing for Children and Young Adults at Vermont College of Fine Arts. She is a citizen of the Muscogee Nation and lives in Austin, Texas. You can visit Cynthia online at cynthialeitichsmith.com.

IN 2014, WE NEED DIVERSE BOOKS (WNDB) began as a simple hashtag on Twitter. The social media campaign soon grew into a 501(c)(3) nonprofit with a team that spans the globe. WNDB is supported by a network of writers, illustrators, agents, editors, teachers, librarians, and book lovers, all united under the same goal—to create a world where every child can see themselves in the pages of a book. You can learn more about WNDB programs at www.diversebooks.org.